YONDER

YONDER

by

MARGARET BELL HOUSTON

Crown Publishers, Inc.

New York

TO KATRINA

Time is not toxic. All those who develop a time neurosis subscribe to the prevalent superstition that time is in some way a poison exerting a mysterious, cumulative action . . . time has no effect on human tissues under any conditions . . . vigor does not necessarily vary inversely with the age of the adult. Belief in the effects of time by those who subscribe to such a belief is the thing which acts as a poison.

From the report of a Conference of medical and surgical specialists at the DeCourcy Clinic in Cincinnati.

YONDER

I

It was raining the night I arrived at Point Muspa. An hour before dusk the train had headed into that rain, borne on a wind that increased in violence as we neared the coast. Not a soul was in sight near the storm-beaten station. The train porter carried my bags inside, and I sat down among them to wait. The station was empty except for the man at the ticket window. He glanced at me now and then. Presently I went over to him.

"Is there any message," I asked, "for Olive York?"

"No, Miss," he said, stacking little slips of paper. "Not yet."

He seemed sorry, seemed to apologize.

"Someone was to have met me," I said. "Someone from Judge Croome's place on Yonder Key."

He looked at me curiously, recovered himself.

"The going's been rough all day," he said. "I don't think the ferry's made a trip since morning."

"Is this a hurricane?" I asked.

He shook his head. "Hurricanes come from the east, out

of the Caribbean. That's their breeding place—blue as a baby's eyes." He turned to his ringing telephone. "No, dear," he answered presently, then, "Yes, dear. Soon."

He was talking to his home, to a sheltered, familiar place that would receive him out of the storm.

"Couldn't we telephone them?" I asked when he was through.

"No phone on the key," he said. "Costs a fortune to lay the cables. I can drive you to a hotel when I lock up here, then in the morning—"

I said that I would wait, and went back to my corner.

I had come from an inland town a thousand miles away. We had storms there, too, loud and black. But this was like a storm at sea. I could hear the sea—that sound of water could not be all rain—and I felt uneasy at being so near it, though all my life I had wanted to live beside ocean or bay, to know them well. That was why I had taken this position on Yonder. That, and Dane.

Dane Carrington had been in my life for twelve years—since I was ten. Perhaps you believe that children, normal children, do not fall in love. I will not dispute with you. I will say only that from the moment I met Dane I belonged to him. He was not aware of his possession, being six years older than I. Between ten and sixteen there is a great gulf fixed. It narrows with the years, but Dane's pursuits were so far apart from mine that he seemed in another world. Besides, I was a plain child—cat's eyes and brown pigtails—quiet, too, made, I am afraid, for the background.

At any rate, in the background I dwelt, alive in every nerve and wishing that I might be melted down, dissolved com-

2

pletely, then poured into some perfect mold to emerge in beauty that would catch Dane's eye. Or else let me be gay and brash, impudent and resourceful, indifferent to any opinion—even his—like his sister Josephine.

Josephine was my best friend. We called her Pony for no reason except that it was not her name. They had a big house with wooded grounds around it, a house full of sunshine and color, of casual comings and goings, with the phone and door-bell always ringing. It was good to be there. In my own house we had often to whisper because Father was having a con-ference in the study.

My mother liked this friendship with Pony whose parents were prominent and respected. Pony's mother liked it, too, for I was a parson's child and Mrs. Carrington had artlessly concluded that my influence would be on the side of the angels. She pinned towering hopes on Pony, wanted her to be discreet and studious then, and later ravishing and a belle.

Pony had freckles and rough red curls. She could climb any fence, wall or tree that ever grew, and she was afraid of nothing except cows. There was a gap between her two front teeth that she could squirt water through to the con-fusion of the family cats and dogs and the envy of her younger brother, Fritz. Besides all this, she had the gift of leadership. In St. Hilda's School, which we both attended, there was a Miss Parr who taught history and who always kept us past the period which was the last half-hour of the day. Pony instructed everybody to bring alarm clocks set for the closing minute. Thirteen alarm clocks going off at once impressed Miss Parr, and though we were all called into the principal's office next day, we got out on the dot after that.

Poor Miss Parr. She avoided Professor Simpkins who taught physics. They said he had squelched her once in a faculty meeting and that she had retaliated in kind. There had followed a series of explosions. Pony sent them each a valentine signed with the other's name. She always said she made that match.

You never knew what Pony was going to do. Brave as she was, she keeled over one day in zoölogy class. The object that upset her was a cat, a campus stray that we had sometimes fed from our lunch baskets, now lying dead and prepared for dissection. I saw Leonie Roy grab her stomach and go out. Then there was a noise and Pony lay on the floor in a dead faint. I didn't have to stay because I was delegated to look after Pony. "It had kittens in it," she gasped as she came to.

Pony wouldn't study. She simply wouldn't study. The instructors used to lecture her about application, about diligence. One of them asked her once if she knew the meaning of routine. Pony said yes, it was French for rut.

Somehow she always got by. She used to cram just before exams and come out by the skin of her teeth.

No, I wouldn't have influenced her, even if I could, I wouldn't have changed her. She was a good leader, and I was a good follower. I followed her as long as I could.

There were three of them, Dane and Pony and Fritz. Dane had charm and a blond, shining, rumpled head that grew smoother as he got older. He played clever, though erratic, tennis, leaping gracefully, white slacks and pastel-colored shirt, gold head bright in the sun. He was fussy about the

4

court. Once he made me take off my shoes and play in my bare feet.

Sometimes he played the piano for us and our friends to dance. When he put his hands on the keys something got into the music that wasn't there before, something limber and rollicking and devil-may-care. You simply couldn't keep still. But he wouldn't practice.

He was lazy in lots of ways like Pony and different from Fritz. Fritz was no mean student, and on Sundays in a white surplice he sang in the choir, looking like a scrubbed angel. Weekdays he played baseball and wore several sweaters at once and brought strange kids home with him. He was always being sent from the table to wash his hands, and once he shaved his head—redder than Pony's—because he was tired of combing it. Now and then he showed up with a black eye, because he'd take on anybody in a fight. Pony used to stand up for him, but Fritz and Dane had no points of contact at all.

Dane never went with us out to the Carrington farm. "There's something about a plow," he said, "that depresses me."

Fritz was happier there than anywhere else, and Pony liked it too, though she had once been chased by a cow. For me, it was heaven. Fields, orchards, smokehouse, dairy and spring. Earth smell. Hay smell. The horse that we called Old Blue, so broad of back that we all three rode him at once, our legs out straight.

Almost as enchanting as the farm was the cottage on the lake where we went for week ends, and where Pony and I learned to swim and paddle and sail. My childhood would have been tame without the Carringtons.

Love takes on wild colors when it seizes the very young. I dreamed of Dane, not only in the night, but often by day. He was the frog in the fairy tale, the frog who turned into a prince and lay beside me in my golden bed while I smoothed his rumpled hair and kissed him. We went on long eventful journeys, by boat, by magic carpet, and we were happy only when we were together.

I was perhaps thirteen then, and I wonder what my mother, reticent in many ways, would have made of my preoccupations. She never suspected them, I am sure, seeing to it that my hair was brushed, my nails clean, my room kept tidy, my lessons learned. It was, of course, reasonable that one's mother should not suspect one's dreams, but I marveled, watching Dane as he sat at dinner or played the piano, that he could share my life so vividly and not know.

Once when he and Pony were both sick with the flu Mrs. Carrington let me help nurse them, let me take in Dane's tray and sit beside him in case he needed anything.

He lay helpless and unhappy, his shining head tousled, his face flushed. He looked at me sullenly when I went in, so that if I had had an impulse to smooth his hair I could not have gratified it. He scowled at the food I brought, and ate little. After taking out the tray I picked up a detective story lying on his night table, found the turned-down leaf—a symbol of independence in my mind, for I had never been allowed to turn down the leaf of any book—and began to read in a low and soothing voice. He flopped over, turning his back, and asked where his mother was.

6

That night I had trouble getting him aboard our adventure-seeking ship, though I knew, having often heard, that all men are cross when they are sick. He went off to college as soon as he got well. I was at the train when he left, and he kissed me good-by.

One summer when he came home there was some mix-up about a girl in the college town he had left. Pony, who was my informant in most matters, told me all she could find out. The girl was a fool, she said, but the girl's family was not. They wanted money. Mr. Carrington swore he wouldn't give them a cent, and Mrs. Carrington said, "Do you want him to marry her?" "It would teach him a lesson," Mr. Carrington replied.

I worried about it a great deal—Dane marrying like that, ignominiously and young, before he had had time to look around. Pony brushed it off. She said nothing bad ever happened to Dane. It was all settled, we never knew how. And pretty soon Dane was home for good, and Pony came out.

Pony wasn't as tame by then as her mother would have liked; another year might have gentled her a lot. As it was, they took her out of school in our senior year, hoping that if they gave her a debut and plenty of excitement she would forget Thad Raeburn. I never thought Pony loved Thad. I believed she found excitement in dating him because their families were at war. Her father and Thad's had been enemies so long they'd forgotten what they first quarreled about. Thad and Pony met in shabby taverns and other people's houses. That was when I stopped following her. I had to. She seemed to dance away down a new road, waving me back. She didn't confide in me any more, though I don't think she had stopped loving me. Dane said she hadn't. He said Thad was a phase, and too serious a guy for Pony.

Pony was nearly nineteen, a year older than I. Her freckles had melted away and she had a wax-white skin, a flaming bob and the prettiest legs I ever saw. Thad, of course, wasn't coming to her party. Her mother would have invited him, but Mr. Carrington was adamant and set his jaw. Pony was going to get back into line or he'd know why. He was in many ways a hard man.

Pony didn't care for the party. She told me I could have it. Mrs. Carrington said, "Olive will certainly share it."

She gave me my dress, made me go along when Pony bought hers and choose one for myself. I say "choose," but I didn't get the one I chose. That was of velvet, a rich, wild red, the color I had always hungered for. I was allowed to try it on, to finger its ardent folds, to wish that it were longer, trailing the floor romantically. Even the most formal dresses of 1925 came to our knees, so that a flapper felt still a flapper when she went to her first ball.

Mrs. Carrington admired the ruby-colored velvet. "But I don't think . . ." She didn't think it was the thing to emerge from a parsonage. "This mist-blue taffeta, dear. It suits you somehow."

Pony's dress was pink tulle, a pale shade, lovely with her red hair, a knowing little dress, for the young, the virgin, adroit in its innocence. Pony had torn its ethereal skirts half off before the party was over, what with her mad dancing and too much punch.

Mrs. Carrington had put me with Dane that night. He came for me, looked after me all evening, and brought me

8

home. Charming, attentive. No doubt his mother had admonished him, "Be nice to Olive. It's her party as well as Pony's." Christmas lights glowed around the doorway and in the trees outside. There was a stringed orchestra, a long shining supper table. I danced with every boy there, I think. They were like shadows lasting only until Dane came and took me away.

Once I ran into Pony on the stair and she squeezed and kissed me. She was laughing, kissing me and laughing. "Olive, darling," she gasped, "if only I could tell you!"

"Tell me what?" I laughed too because *she* was laughing.

"Something thrilling," she said, and nearly fell, teetering and laughing on the top step.

I begged, but she pulled away and ran on down the hall. I didn't follow. Perhaps it would have made no difference if I had. I let her go, and went on down to have another dance with Dane.

It was years before I saw her again. She met Thad Raeburn in the grounds that night and ran away with him. All week I helped her mother pack her things. Mrs. Carrington was crying most of the time, trying to discover what Pony had taken with her. The brown suit and hat, the pigskin bag. We found the tulle dress on the floor of her room, and a note pinned to the floppy French doll on her chaise longue. "I love you all," it said. "Olive doesn't know a thing."

They had left for Venezuela where Thad had taken a job with an oil company.

"Foolish, foolish children," wept Mrs. Carrington. "What will become of them?"

What would become of Pony?

The last semester of school was dull without her.

II

Father called on the poor, the sick, the sinful, and they called
on him. Always in the study there was some desperate parent,
or frightened widow, or girl in tears. There is drama in a
parsonage, but it is always the last act only, the dregs, the
grimy backwash of what has once been freedom or fun.

In my room next to the study I could hear these voices, the
visitor's disturbed accents and Father's deep murmur, com-
forting, quieting. If anything could be done, Father would
do it. It might be the closing of a breach between husband
and wife—he always said that unless the breach had been
caused by nagging on the part of one of them it could be
closed; or it might be the finding of a place where a child
could be born out of wedlock as secretly as possible. Sometimes there would be long distance calls. Always there would
be prayer. One night I heard Mrs. Carrington's voice, low,
and so troubled that it haunted me for days.

Father looked like an archangel with his finely modeled
face, his noble head and dark eyes. His voice in the pulpit,
warm and rich and full of chords, moved me so that, sitting

in the corner of our pew, my throat ached and I swallowed tears. Women must have loved him when he was young. They loved him still. Mother got upset at times. She saw things he didn't see, being abstracted.

Mother knew female strategy, having used it herself. A siren with ringlets (to judge by her photographs), she had wanted Father and she got him—had played the organ in church, washed the altar linen with her own white hands, sought his advice and asked his prayers, made a violet satin cover for his sermons, confident that she would be a good wife for a struggling young divine.

Well, she was, though never so active in church work as before she married, and never free of coquetry. I remember the last hat she bought. "Where shall I place the rose?" asked the milliner. "Toward the congregation," my mother replied.

Father's sermons were good, down to earth for all his abstraction. And the impractical things he did—which were many—had a disconcerting way of turning out all right. When he gave away his overcoat another always found its way to him. The same with money. Somebody would pay an old debt, or maybe just think about him and send him a check. Mother needn't have worried.

He believed the church should heal sickness as well as sin. He was not alone in this, even then, but that was a cross to Mother, too. She knew that Jesus said, "Heal the sick," and "The things that I do ye shall do also." "But he was speaking to his disciples, not to you," said Mother.

"He also said, 'These signs shall follow them that believe . . . they shall lay hands on the sick and they shall recover,' " Father answered. "Perhaps you don't know that in the second century, in the time of Irenaeus, even the raising of the dead was not uncommon. Then spirituality in the church declined. It must be regained."

"You're only one man," said Mother. "What can you do?" Plainly she felt it eccentric.

However, she profited by his faith. Once when she was very ill, and the doctor said she might not recover, Father sent me away from her side. Afterward it grew so still in their room that I stole back and opened the door. Father sat with the Bible open before him, his head bowed. There was a light in the room, not just the little light above the pages of the Bible, but a strange bright glow all through the room. Mother didn't know anything about it. She was unconscious. But next day she was well. She never opposed him after that.

And there was the child who came out of convulsions while he prayed. And the man who was healed of blindness during one of his sermons. There were healings of chronic disease, of poverty and sorrow. Our church was crowded.

Prayer should never fail, he said. The Bible was full of unplumbed riches, of passages with power.

Love. The perfect love that casts out fear. Faith that is the absence of fear. The prayer of faith shall save the sick. How often Jesus said, *"Thy faith* hath saved thee." Faith takes you a long way.

But a law, he said, underlay all the miracles of the Old and New Testaments, a law as invariable as mathematics, as ever-operative and infallible. Back of faith, back of love—the law, the hidden wisdom spoken of by Paul.

Ye shall know the truth and the truth shall make you free.
Give me understanding, and I shall live.

12

I was tutoring then, three nights a week. Fritz Carrington was one of my pupils. Fritz had been conditioned in Latin and English. We used to work in the old playroom, and afterward Dane would drive me home. Often on winter evenings he would come inside, and we'd sit by the fire and talk. Sometimes Father joined us, and Mother briefly, bringing coffee and Brenda's fragrant little cakes.

Father enjoyed talking with Dane. He said the boy had a mind if he would use it. I'm sure he used it at the bank. He had gone into his father's bank as soon as he came home for good.

College had given Dane some new ideas, ideas that interested me because they were different from anything I had ever heard. I thought, however, he was bold airing them in his discussions with Father. For instance, he said that prayer was the opiate of the masses. Startling. Revolutionary. Where had he got that? Prayer an opiate.

"Let's hope it's habit-forming," said Father.

Dane remarked later to me that he shouldn't talk shop with a parson.

He shouldn't indeed. He should say these extraordinary things only to me who listened and weighed them and had no embarrassing rejoinders.

We were alone when he said that marriage was eugenically wrong. Father might have tried to set him right. Me, I was willing to learn.

"Why?" I asked.

"Natural children," he answered. "Love children, as they are called, are always more intelligent and better formed."

"Is there a reason?"

"It lies in the word 'natural.' They are not born of habit and convenience. Hadn't you thought of that?"

I hadn't, of course. But this was deep talk.

"There's something very perfunctory and premeditated about marriage," he said.

"You don't believe in it?"

"I admit," he replied, "that things might grow confused without it. When we give nature her head she doesn't always cooperate with civilization."

"Or the home," I added.

" 'Home' is one of the sentimental words," he said. "The Spaniards haven't got it, and they get along fine. 'Little' is another. Look at what it does to 'child.' To 'old lady.' "

"I'd say it had affection."

"It's a sniveling word. Lots of adjectives are. Words are entities, they can have a weakening effect racially. Take the word 'mother.' We could manage without it."

"How about 'father'?"

"It will do. Not so mawkish as 'mother.' "

"But I'm more mawkish about my father than I am about my mother."

"You're a sassy pupil. And decadent when it comes to words. Never, for instance, say a guy's noble. It's purest corn."

"Suppose he *is* noble."

"Spare me. And if I ever catch you saying 'tender' except in reference to beefsteak, or 'golden' instead of 'gold,' or 'blossom—' "

"I think blossom is a beautiful word."

"Beauty's done for, darlin'. This is the age of realism, lusty and naked and stark. I'm tellin' you."

"Father," I said, "beauty's done for. This is the age of realism. Dane said so."

" 'Weep for Adonais, he is dead,' " smiled Father. "A hundred years ago Flaubert said the time for beauty was over. It's still around, not in realism, perhaps, but in reality. Realism varies with the plane we live on. It's one thing to the mole, another to the lark. Reality is truth, and 'truth beauty. That is all ye know on earth, and all ye need to know.' "

"Dane," I said, "beauty is not done for. Flaubert said it was out a hundred years ago, but it's still around. Maybe not in art," I added on my own, "but in nature. Even in people. Some are beautiful on the inside, some on the outside."

And I thought, nothing could be so beautiful as you, with the sun in your hair. He was driving me to the parish house where the choirboys' minstrel show was in rehearsal.

"What am I going to do with you," he said, "when you go off and cogitate, and come back at me like that? How am I going to train you?"

"Train me for what?"

"For life. This parsonage is not doing it . . . Belong to your racial group, Olive. Be light. Be brittle. Don't think so much. Don't feel."

I don't want to be brittle, I thought. . . . Eggshells. Crackers. Dry sticks and dead leaves . . . Brittleness seemed more an absence of traits than a trait . . . Light, yes. Light and gay like Pony. That perhaps I might be, or affect to be. But let me who still brought home stray dogs and worried about birds on winter nights, who, like Maggie in *The Mill on the Floss,* could never get enough music at once except when the pipe organ played—let me who felt an ocean inside her, an ocean with no outlet (Oh to be a musician like Dane!)—let me hide my full ignominy from those amused eyes.

Sometimes when he was in the mood he sat down at the old parsonage piano and played eerie bits from the ballet he was composing.

"It's wonderful, Dane. Don't just bury and forget it the way you did 'The Dance of the Night Herons.' "

"Do you remember that?"

A memory of his childhood made into music. Once in Florida he had seen the night herons dance. Beauty . . . beauty . . . beauty . . .

"Of course I remember it," I said. "Don't you?"

"I'm afraid not," half seeking it along the keys. "Pretty young stuff."

"Learn it again," I said, "and play it for me."

Oh to inspire him, to goad him into making the most of his music.

Sometimes we talked about girls, and so I kept in touch with his fleeting romances. . . . Did he love anyone at all, I wondered. Did he even hate? Was there anything he wanted? Had he an ambition, a goal, that was not too easily attained?

The ripe, immediate pleasure, to pluck and savor it, and cast away the hull. Skimming the surface of life, a bright-winged bird, singing his own song. Nothing to bind the foot,

16

nothing that looked like a cage. Intrigued by the devices of escape rather than of pursuit.

People were beginning to say that I looked like Father, that I had his voice, words that pleased me. Love knocked at my door in various guises, but was not for me. I was Dane's captive. Like a lady in a tower I watched my days go by, quiet nuns marching to what place I could not foretell. Busy days. Our house was big for a parsonage, roomy and comfortable, with good cupboards and a fine old Colonial mantel in the living room.

I was housekeeper now with the help of Brenda, sturdy maid-of-all-work provided by the parish. I also typed Father's sermons and many of his letters, helped at the parish house, and worked with Mother in the flower garden, a somewhat neglected place till she had arrived.

The aphids I've slain under her direction, the delphiniums I've staked, the buds I've pinched off strawberry plants—to me, the garden was not a lovesome spot, God wot. Not always. But Mother's passion for it flamed from the first shivering crocus till the lawn mower was cleaned and put in the cellar. Tirelessly she knelt among the flower beds, dividing the phlox, pruning the small shrubs, setting out bulbs. She wore big gloves to protect her hands, and a wide straw hat to ward off tan.

Often we had breakfast at the iron table under the beech tree. I loved the garden then, felt flooded with happiness, rich in bliss. Life seemed complete, here at its golden core. It was ecstasy merely to be alive, with the spirea in bloom and the birds back again, and Brenda plodding stolidly over the flagstones with the eggs and coffee.

After breakfast Mother would put flowers on Father's desk, and look over his list of calls and duties for the day, and wipe away any bit of dust overlooked by Brenda and me. When she wasn't in the garden she was sewing—replacing Father's buttons, yanked off in the wash by Brenda; darning his socks, hemming napkins and cup towels—the supply seemed endless. Once a week she would have Brenda make pyramids of sandwiches ("I wouldn't cut off the crusts, myself," said Brenda to me, "but your mother wants things refined.") and have the young folks of the parish in to tea. We had fun on those occasions, though they wouldn't have come and drunk tea anywhere else, a fact that never occurred to Mother. She would speak afterwards of any boy that had seemed to single me out. "He'd make a good husband," she'd say. "If I were a girl . . ."

She would have liked to live her youth again in me, to see me marry and have children.

"You're a frustrated grandmother," I said to her once.

"And you, dear," she sighed, "are unnatural."

I had merely not been broken enough to compromise.

Suddenly everything changed.

Father had a young curate, Andrew Simms, who took much of the visiting off his hands. One Fourth of July Mrs. Carrington invited Andrew and me to a moonlight picnic out at the lake. "There won't be a moon," she said, "till late. But so much the better. We're having fireworks."

Andrew was a somber person, so silent for the most part

18

that I wondered why Mrs. Carrington had thought he would add anything to her picnic. As it turned out, he added a great deal, helping to unpack the baskets, and lifting an earnest tenor when we all sang to somebody's ukulele. People always go native at picnics. I guess it comes of sitting on the ground. I missed Pony that night more than I had ever missed her. It seemed to be part of an ominous feeling I had had all day, as if something were about to happen, an accident maybe. I told Andrew about it before we started, said I didn't want to go. He said, "Nonsense. If you give way to things like that, they'll take possession of you."

Dane had brought a girl I hadn't seen in years. Leonie Roy. I had known her at St. Hilda's where she used to board when her parents went abroad, which was often, Mr. Roy being an importer of textiles. In those days Leonie had been a pale, rather listless girl, with small bird bones and dark eyes too big for her face. People were always doing things for her, making her bed, writing her compositions, running her errands. Not that she asked these things of anyone. You merely knew they needed to be done, and that she couldn't or wouldn't do them. Besides that, there was something appealing about her. I remember once drawing a map of Asia for Leonie because her brother was coming to take her to the ball game, and she had to dress.

She had grown up to her eyes now, was still pale and slight, with a painted cherry of a mouth, and beautiful eyelids feathered in long lashes. Her movements, the tilt of her head, were like a bird's, like a ballerina's. She and Dane sat with Andrew and me at supper. Something in the way Dane looked at her, in the way she took him for granted . . . No wonder I'd seen very little of Dane lately.

Was she light and brittle? I thought not. In spite of much lingering in Paris there was something almost demure about her—that droop of the head as she looked at you from beneath her fabulous lashes. She spoke, too, with the slight lisp I remembered from St. Hilda's.

"Isn't she wonderful?" Dane said in an aside to me.

I repeated the all-enveloping word.

"Wonderful. She's one you never told me about."

"I've just discovered her. Do you approve?"

"I must think it over." I smiled. "When is it to be?"

"Soon, I hope. Yes, soon."

Dane and Leonie vanished after supper, went out on the lake in a canoe. That was when Andrew was useful with the fireworks. Mrs. Carrington had depended on Dane.

The ukulele was still now. There was a dark hush. Then came the long hiss as the first rocket winged into the sky, pouring a golden, a jeweled shower over lake and treetops, revealing them in an instant's magic light, leaving them in blackness. Again and again, fountains and geysers exploding among the stars, millions of flowers, of fireflies, of rainbow streamers, drifting, dissolving . . .

Out on the lake Dane and Leonie would have an even better view. But perhaps they were not watching at all.

At home that night I lay with the skyey fountains still in my eyes, with the blackness that came afterward.

III

Father was going to the Convention in California, and he was taking Mother. Mother hadn't had a trip in years, and made no effort to hide her excitement. There were two new dresses and a new hat. The parish was excited, too, and brought presents, though the depression was under way. Airplane luggage, and a fur stole for Mother on cool evenings.

I drove them to the airport and found Andrew part of a company already there to see them off. Mother said as Andrew came toward us, "A nice young man. He'd make a good husband." She spoke absently, was a bit breathless at sight of the plane, and conscious of her new faille dress and the hat with the rose on it. Father looked calm and distinguished, saying a few parting words to Andrew, to everyone. In his briefcase was his paper on Spiritual Healing in the Churches which I had been typing for him all week. He had been advised by some not to read it. They felt that his research had carried him too far afield. But Father felt, and said in his paper, that whatever book threw light on the Scripture was his meat. "Our religion is dynamic," he wrote, "and we seem to be afraid of it. We need the courage of the scientist, the spirit of adventure."

One more hug, one more kiss, as if they were traveling to China itself, but flying was not the casual thing then that it is today. Mother said, "I don't think there'll be a freeze while I'm gone, but if there's any sign of it, bring in my begonias."

Good-by. They turned on the step and waved, smiling happily like two children going to a party. The plane went down the runway, lifted its great weight, climbed into the blue, its nose pointing westward. Some of us watched till it was no larger than a bird, till it became a star and vanished.

Andrew got into the car with me. He was troubled, and I knew it was about Father's paper. Andrew was not opposed to healing work in the Church, but he felt it should be done in association with psychiatrists and physicians. I let him out at the parish house and went marketing. Miss Lora Whitley who worked in the public library was going to spend the week with me. Brenda always went home at night and everybody felt I should not be alone in the house. Miss Lora was a vegetarian. That made it hard . . . Stuffed eggplant, I decided, would be the main dish that night. And there was a macaroni casserole that wasn't bad, and egg Tetrazzini that had to do with mushrooms and Parmesan cheese. I planned the week's menu as I wandered about the market, running into friends, selecting fruit and vegetables with Miss Lora in mind.

It was late when I got home. Brenda hadn't come to get dinner. The house felt empty, and I went out to the kitchen and began to make a salad. I wished for a small portable radio to enliven things, then realized that I might turn on the big radio in the living room and set it at full strength. It seemed strange, however, wild and outrageous—the radio blaring like that when Father might be working in the study. Jazz booming through the house when Father might be consoling someone in trouble.

The jazz was interrupted by a bulletin.

My life stopped that day. Stopped to resume, of course, but as a different life, bearing on its current a little of the old freight, bearing me, a different person.

I had wondered how I would endure a great sorrow, a great shock. Now I knew. Yet at first I would not let it in. It was only a voice interrupting a jazz orchestra to shout that a plane was in trouble, a plane was overdue, a plane had crashed.

All night I hung over the radio with Miss Lora, with Brenda till she was forced to go home. All night the phone rang, people came and went. Some one said, "You are brave." I was not brave. I had simply not taken it in. It was at noon the next day that I realized they would not come back, that they lay in a mass of burned wreckage on a remote mountainside, just now reached by rescuers who found no one alive. I remembered the pilot, lean, dark-eyed, smoking a cigarette before he climbed into his seat. I remembered the young father who was taking his children to visit their grandmother. I could see again all the faces that had looked at us from the plane, could see the two standing on the steps, smiling, waving. I saw these things even when my eyes were closed. The radio that had funneled the world into our living room, a hitherto impersonal voice, began to speak intimately to me alone. The faces crowded about my bed, shifting, blending, changing, in the dark.

Miss Lora came to my door that second night and asked for another blanket; it was turning cold . . . The blankets, I thought. Where are the blankets? Where do we keep them?

Miss Lora found the blankets in the cedar cupboard, spread one over me. "Go to sleep, dear child." She took her blanket and went back to her room.

It was turning cold. There would be a freeze, perhaps.

What was it I must bring in, what was it I must find? I went out on the back porch, searching, groping in the wet black dark . . . It would be in the garden. The steps, the flagstones were slippery. It was sleeting. I was in my nightgown. My hair was getting wet . . . I felt among the chrysanthemums, bowed under the sleet. I felt along the wall.

Brenda, coming early, found me huddled under the beech tree. I remember very little after that. Of the days that followed I remember nothing at all.

I lay in bed, looking out the window. I could remember that night in the garden and all that went before, but I thought these things had happened yesterday. However, this could not be, for then the maples were blazing red, and now they were full of snow. I thought, I have been ill, but Father and Mother will never know. They soared into the sky. They will not turn back . . . What was it Dane said? Don't think. Don't feel.

Mrs. Carrington sat beside the window, reading. Her hair was a lighter red than Fritz's but deeper than Pony's. I wondered if Dane was married yet, but when his mother rose and came over to me I asked only, "Has Pony written?"

She put pillows behind me and helped me to sit up. She gave me a packet of mail, but only a cable of condolence, very old, was from Pony.

"You know she never writes," Mrs. Carrington said.

It was true. Pony, at best, had written only brief notes, mere pleas to visit her. Her mother had received such messages, too, and had wanted to go and take me with her, but Mr. Carrington had forbidden it. He was not a man you could wheedle.

Besides the letters there were packages, Christmas presents. One was from Pony, a bed jacket of orchid satin. A card with Pony's scrawl. "Get well fast. Love. . . . P.S. I made the jacket."

I asked Mrs. Carrington to put it on me. Pony's stitches.

A vase of carnations stood on a table near the door. All morning I had been conscious of their clovey, hothouse smell. Now, sitting up, I saw them, tall and pink.

"From Dane," Mrs. Carrington said. "Open your presents, dear, and read your letters. It's Christmas Day."

In another week I needed no one to nurse me. Brenda was there, and always some woman friend came to be with me at night. And now the parsonage must be made ready for its new occupants. Those things that had belonged to us—Mother's wedding silver, the old chest-on-chest and fruitwood table, Father's books—I planned to store. Their clothes I would give to charity. Mrs. Carrington had packed them while I was in the hospital.

I did not remember the hospital, did not remember coming home. Groping back, I seemed to enter a red twilight filled with ghosts of delirium, of pain and smothering. I must not grope back . . . Don't think. Don't feel.

Mrs. Carrington asked me one day if I had any plans. Mother had left me stock in a lumber mill—nothing spectacular—and I had Father's small insurance. Mr. Carrington was Father's executor, and was later to give me good advice.

It occurred to me that I could travel, pay alone that long promised visit to Pony in Caracas. Mrs. Carrington was silent when I mentioned this. Then she said that Pony was by now in Paris. Pony's elopement no longer seemed an adventure, and she was restless. Never in one place very long.

The idea of joining Pony faded like a comet from my mind. When Mrs. Carrington spoke again of my future I said that I could teach at St. Hilda's or maybe marry Andrew Simms who had asked me more than once. I had never thought of marrying Andrew, yet the idea seemed a familiar one, as if it had been lying behind some door in my mind. For one thing, he had been thoughtful during my convalescence, bringing me broth his mother had made, and woolly socks to sleep in. Besides, it would be good to have a person of one's own, and Mother had said just as she was leaving that Andrew would make . . .

"You can't decide while you're still weak," Mrs. Carrington said. "Just think things over."

And she told me about Yonder Key where I might go, if I liked, and be a sort of companion to her cousin.

"They've asked me to look around for someone here. The work's not hard, and the salary's good. It would be a change."

Yonder Key. It was like living in a shell, she said, with the sound of the sea all around. Blue coral on the beach, and pink seaweed. And the sea where it shallowed up to the land every color of the rainbow.

She hadn't been back in more than twenty years, though Point Muspa on the near mainland had been her home till she married. I hadn't known this, hadn't known that she had ever lived anywhere else. She had never spoken of these relatives, and I had the feeling that she spoke of them now only because of her wish to help me.

"Since Zoé got ill," she said, "my uncle and Johanna, the other daughter, have shut themselves away from the world. That sort of thing changes people. I wouldn't enjoy visiting them now. Zoé, herself, when I saw her last, wasn't at all depressing. You wouldn't guess there was anything wrong. I might have liked being with her if I hadn't known the thing that happened to her, that robbed her of her reason, and made them all—"

Mrs. Carrington stopped suddenly, and something like a veil dropped over her face.

"I wouldn't want you to stay more than a year," she said presently. "Not even that, if you were not happy. But the quiet of the place, and the sea air— I almost envy you. We had good times when we were girls, Zoé and I. Wild, I guess, for our generation, but Johanna kept us in line. You probably won't see much of Johanna. I understand she's ill—physically, that is—confined to her room. You'd just be with Zoé, and you'd have the sun and the ocean and everything new."

27

In my mail the day after Christmas I had found the invitation to Dane's wedding, set for January seventh. I could be far away by then . . . There was a sedative in that thought of the sea . . .

"Fritz and I will miss you," Dane's mother said.

IV

On New Year's Day the door knocker sounded abruptly. Brenda wasn't due that day, and I sat alone before a one-egg omelet and a cup of tea, commanding myself to eat.

Twice that sound of the door knocker. I was expecting Jean Thomas who was spending the night, and I went to the door on the chance that it might be Jean, though I had on a house-dress and no girdle and my hair was tumbled.

It was Dane. Dane in the late winter afternoon, with the glow of the cold on his face. Dark overcoat and crimson muffler. Bare bright head.

I stood looking at him.

"Can't I come in?" He laughed.

"Oh, Dane, of course. How stupid of me."

But when the door was closed he said, "It's stuffy in here. Get on your things. I'll take you sleighing."

It was like a dream. He helped me into my coat, into woolen gloves and parka and fur-lined boots. "We'll put some color in your face," he said.

We left the key under the mat for Jean.

It was an old-fashioned sleigh with an old-fashioned horse, Asa, son of Old Blue whom Pony and Fritz and I had ridden all at once on the farm. Asa had on the collar with the bells and there were strips of bells along the shafts. We jingled off under the frozen maples, over the hard white road, through a white world . . . A dream, yes. The whiteness, the sleigh, the jingling bells. Dane . . . The cold stung my face. I felt exhilarated, electric. I forgot that in a week Dane would be married.

"What do you mean, getting sick?" he demanded. "What do you mean scaring everybody like that?"

"I'm all right now," I assured him, sitting up straight.

I was getting my bearings. His mother, I knew, had said to him, "Olive will probably be gone when you and Leonie get back. Go say good-by to her."

The sleigh ride, of course, was his own idea.

I said, "Thank you for the flowers. And for the invitation, too. I had to believe it when I saw that."

He smiled his delightful smile.

"You don't know Leonie, do you?"

"I used to, though not well."

"We'll change all that. You're going to know each other, like each other."

So that was settled.

"Turn your face around. Yep, you're looking better. There's a rose in your cheek. Two roses . . . Where do you want to go?"

I thought of the farm three miles out, but said, "Anywhere."

We were in a street of little houses. Decorated trees

twinkled through the windows, holly wreaths still hung on doors. We skirted the lake, drove past the country club. A gray New Year's with a feeling of more snow.

"Comfortable, Olive?"

"Oh, yes!"

"I hope you're dressed warm underneath . . . So grave, so serious. The white flower of the parsonage, rooted in the eternal verities. What are you thinking about?"

"About the green pants Pony used to wear when we went sleighing. It seemed when we started out—I mean just the first minute—that Fritz and Pony were with us. Wasn't that crazy? . . . Do you remember those pants?"

"Gosh, yes. They revolted me. I hate girls in pants."

"Then you do hate something."

"What do you mean, I do hate something? I hate lots of things. Short hair on women is another."

The merits of bobbed hair were still debated in 1930.

"Why do they do it?" asked Dane. "Why do they make their heads like men's heads?"

"Why do men shave?" I asked. "Why do they make their faces like women's faces?"

"Now that's a thought. Anyhow, I'm glad Leonie still has her hair. You lost your mystery when you cut yours."

I thought of the amber silk curtain of Leonie's hair.

"Did I have mystery, Dane?"

"Yes, certainly. Even as a kid."

"Because of pigtails?"

"Pigtails and round yellow-gray eyes sizing people up. And listening. Always the good listener, so that people told you more than they intended. Mysterious. Like a little owl."

31

"Owls aren't mysterious. They're just dumb."

"That's a libel. We see owls only by day when they're asleep. In the dark when they make those weird noises and swoop down on their prey they're anything but dumb. Fasten your collar. How do you feel now?"

"Weird. Mysterious . . . Dane, were you ever on Yonder Key?"

"Once. When I was a kid. Mother took Pony and me. Pony was a baby. We stayed all winter."

"That was when you saw the herons dance."

He smiled, seeming to humor me, tucked the bear robe around me. "Yes. That was when I saw the herons."

"Did you like Yonder?" I asked.

"Yes. The beach was fine. The rest was queer."

"Queer?"

"Not the island. The people. The family, the whole bunch. They weren't supposed to be, but they were. Balmy."

"I know about Zoé," I said.

"Yes, Zoé was balmy. But keen. Gave me her toys. We went to see her up a long stair, several stairs, I think. I could have taken her toys home with me, but Mother made me give them back. I used to play on the beach all day, digging, wading, watching the gulls. Yes, I liked Yonder."

"Was Johanna queer?"

"Well, nobody said so, but I used to want to hide from her eyes. She's good-looking though—even I could see that. Shining black hair. Once I saw her brushing it. It came to her knees. The old man and I were right good friends, but looking back I can see he was queer as the rest . . . You aren't actually going there, are you?"

32

"I might. Do you advise against it?"

"I'd say your alternatives were better. St. Hilda's, I mean, or the Reverend Simms."

So his mother had told him about that.

"You'd make a fine wife for a parson, Olive. A natural. My family, by the way, would like to have you live with them, take Pony's place. But Mother thinks the town has too many associations for you, thinks you should fly to ills you know not of. Maybe she's right."

He flecked the whip, and Asa quickened his trot.

"How do you feel now, Olive?"

"Fine, fine."

Again the fleck of the whip.

"Think I'll take you home now. Asa won't need any urging when we've rounded the curve . . . Yes, go on to Yonder, Olive. It's probably different now. Gee, that was more than twenty years ago. Cousin Johanna's old now. So is Zoé. I never thought about that before . . ."

It was snowing hard. Twilight was falling, and there was the glimmer of Christmas lights on the lawns. Snow was falling, too, into my lap, clinging to Dane's gloved hand as it held the reins. Words with no meaning swam through my mind, mixed with the jingling bells and the words Dane was saying a great way off. Dane's words were far away, but his shoulder was close, and comforted me. Suddenly I heard him call my name and tried to answer. I couldn't, but it didn't matter. Nothing mattered.

Nothing seemed still to matter when I opened my eyes again and saw, in the darkening twilight, familiar indoor things—the wall clock, the rows of books, the desk, the green-upholstered chair.

I lay among the pillows of the study couch, and Dane sat on the couch beside me. I could smell wine, taste wine. The pillow was wet. Dane's face bent above me. I seemed to look up at his face from the bottom of a well.

"Are you all right?" he asked.

His face wavered and floated, a face seen through water.

I heard my voice.

"Did I faint?"

"Dead away. We were almost at your gate."

He had taken off my coat and parka and the fur-lined boots. They lay on the floor beside a broken wineglass.

"You knew what to do . . . You found the wine . . ."

It was hard to talk, to whisper, and be heard from the bottom of a well.

"Wine's always on sideboards," he answered. "I'd no idea the fresh air would hurt you. I thought it would make you well."

"It did. This is nothing."

How shining his eyes were, though it was almost night in the room. Blue eyes with dark pupils. I had never seen them like that, dark yet bright.

The shining eyes came closer. His cheek touched mine. I closed my eyes, and his kiss found my eyelids, moved down to my mouth, kindling and pressing hard. I had dreamed of kissing Dane, yet not kisses like those. I lay drinking that un-imagined bliss, having no will but his. He drew me against him, and with some alien strength my arms pressed him closer still. His heart beat, fought, against mine.

"Olive! Oh, Olive!"

I thought, When I'm dying I'll hear that cry.

It stopped. He held me still, but he seemed to be listening. I heard it, too, the front door knocker sounding frantically.

"Let them knock." His whisper against my face.

"It's Jean," I whispered back. "She's come to spend the night."

Jean Thomas out in the snow. Not getting an answer, not finding the key, she would rouse the neighborhood.

He released me and rose, stood for a moment, then lit a cigarette, smoothed his hair and went out into the hall. A wave of cold air rushed in as he opened the front door. I heard him telling Jean how I had fainted, how he had brought me home.

She asked, "Have you called the doctor?"

A moment later she breezed into the study. "Lie still, Olive." She put on the light, picked up the telephone.

I knew that in the hall Dane was getting into his overcoat. The front door closed. He was gone.

Jean put me to bed in my own room. I heard her ask the doctor if a relapse was worse than the original sickness.

A nurse came. I said, "If I'm going to be sick, I want to be sick in the study."

That was where the telephone was.

They made up the study couch and moved me to it, the

35

phone on a low table in easy reach. If Dane called, I would be there to answer. Perhaps he had called already, and they had not told me. He was sure to have called. He would call again.

Dane was mine. I lived over and over again the moments when he had held and kissed me, so that my temperature worried both doctor and nurse . . . Had those moments been a shock to Dane as they were to me, revealing as they did the fact that he loved me?

When the phone rang I answered it, but it was never Dane. Never Dane when the door knocker sounded.

Only Mrs. Carrington or Jean.

Never the right flowers, only Andrew's.

Andrew came and sat beside me.

"You need a keeper, Olive. Out sleighing in a snowstorm. Just up from pneumonia, and sleighing in a snowstorm. What Dane Carrington was thinking of—"

Oh, go away. Go away.

"Here's a new book, Olive. I haven't had time to read it, but my mother liked it. *Swan Song* by Galsworthy. Would you like me to read to you?"

"No, Andrew. Please."

I thought of Dane turning his back on me when he had flu. How horrible I must have been, reading to him. What a bore.

Tomorrow was Dane's wedding day.

Andrew went at last and I picked up the telephone, calling the bank, asking for the extension that meant Dane's desk.

"Hello!" Dane's voice. "Hello!" he said.

I pressed the mouthpiece against my breast, listening to his voice. "Hello! . . ."

He cradled the receiver.

"The girl was a fool," Pony had said, oh how long ago.

The girl was a fool.

There was another snowstorm, almost a blizzard, the day I left. Mrs. Carrington was taking her turn with the flu, and Fritz saw me to the train. Andrew and Jean were at the station. Andrew had bought our car, and they had come in that. Sounded cozy. Maybe they'd start going together, I thought, reminding myself of Mother.

Mrs. Carrington had given me a pigskin bag like Pony's, and a strand of amber beads she had worn as a girl.

"Good-by, dear," she said. "It's a mercy flight you're going on. Don't take with you anything you won't need. Put everything else behind you and shut the door. Try to forget."

Forget. Forget that those who made my life are gone. They will not return. Forget that Dane is on his honeymoon, that he went without a word or sign. Forget the night he married when I wished I had never been born, or at least that he had never kissed me alive . . . Dane is dead. Dead to me. He was mine, or might have been—for an hour, a night . . . Dane is dead. Bury him.

I had no life at all when I went to Yonder.

V

The hands of the station clock pointed to midnight. I was setting the watch on my wrist when the outer door opened and a man blew in. He shut the door with difficulty, then, glancing about the room, came toward me. He was young, under thirty certainly, dressed in a wet macintosh and a nautical-looking hat that scattered rain as he took it off. Dark hair. Dark eyes. A somewhat disarming smile.

"Miss York? I'm Richard Lowrie. Judge Croome asked me to meet you. I'm sorry to be so late."

"The storm," I said.

"Yes, it caught me down the coast. Fortunately, the ferry's been held up, too. It's waiting a few more minutes for us."

He was gathering up my bags. There had been no sign of a porter anywhere.

I said goodnight to the ticket agent who spoke also to my guide, and we went through the door and along the platform to a waiting car. Richard Lowrie stored my bags in the tonneau, and opened the front door that I might sit beside him. What his position was in the Croome family—friend, relative, employee—I did not know. In our close shelter we breasted the storm while the windshield wiper labored against the driving rain. I could see fitfully the glimmer of the town, and presently the docks with, beyond them, a crashing, booming darkness that was my first glimpse of the sea. We moved aboard the ferry, a lantern-lit cave. I saw no other cars. The ferry began to move, and the charging black waves lunged against it, drenching the deck.

"Rather a gale," Richard Lowrie said.

"It's not a hurricane?"

"No, this isn't the season. Just a squall that we may find worse on Yonder. Judge Croome said yesterday that you were to go straight to bed tonight and meet the family tomorrow."

Welcome words. Bed after a hot bath. I knew I would sleep tonight, even with the wind blowing, and the sea all around.

We were on land again. The ferry dissolved into the storm, making its way toward other keys. We toiled again through blackness along a road swimming in rain. Our headlights picked out the distraught shapes of trees, lost them again. The storm was noisier here, screaming and beating against our sealed windows. We had left the sea, now we were beside it again.

"That's the Atlantic out there," Richard Lowrie said. "You crossed Muspa Bay."

We arrived at iron gates, thoughtfully left open. I saw a sweep of driveway, lashing palm trees, the stone façade of a house. We stopped in a porte-cochère and my guide helped me out. His ring brought no answer, and he took out a key and opened the door.

We stood in a baronial hall. Overhead a chandelier dropped a subdued light on gray walls and stone floors, on draperies and tapestries and carved high-backed chairs. A place of gloom and shadow, like a vault, like a prison. You couldn't hear the storm now. We had left it behind, had entered a place of quiet, and of fog, less seen than felt.

Down the hall a man in a white coat was coming toward us. He was no longer young, but he walked with a singular erectness, an even, gliding walk, completely without hurry. His skin was dark, and his features as nearly perfect as any I had ever seen. There was something strangely arresting about this servant, and I watched him while he looked at Richard Lowrie, awaiting his orders, seeming not to see me at all.

"Good evening, Ezra. Get Miss York's bags out of the car and take them up to her room." Richard Lowrie turned to me. "Would you like something hot to drink before you turn in?"

"Coffee," I answered gratefully.

"Ezra will bring it to your room," he said.

We went up the stair and along an upper hall toward what appeared to be the front of the house. Deep-piled rugs hushed our feet, we could not have disturbed anyone. Ezra came presently, bringing my bags, guiding us to a room where a night lamp burned. Richard Lowrie said goodnight, hoping I would sleep well.

I closed the door and looked about me.

Massive furniture and faded moss-green carpet. Long inside shutters locked against the storm which I could hear again, beating and wailing. A fire was almost dead in the stone fireplace. There was an odor of mold and camphor. The immense bed had been turned down, and the door of the bathroom left open.

I had taken off my hat and my damp coat when I heard a knock. The coffee, I thought, and opened the door.

It was Ezra, but without the coffee. He looked at me now, and said in a voice without inflection that Miss Johanna wished to see me . . . Miss Johanna. My patient's sister . . . Judge Croome's message had been that I would meet the family tomorrow. Perhaps Miss Johanna did not know this.

I turned to a mirror and smoothed my rumpled hair, then followed Ezra downstairs. Off the main hall he entered a dim stone passage and knocked on a door.

Johanna Croome sat in a wheel chair. A thin, large-boned woman with iron-gray hair neatly arranged, and fine black eyes. Her skin had the gray indoor look of a mushroom, and there were hollows beneath her high cheekbones. She wore a long black dress that concealed her feet, and there were diamonds at her throat and on her hands.

"Sit down, Miss York," she said in a deep voice.

The room was a small parlor, or perhaps I should say library, for there were many shelves of books between the shuttered windows. Little sound of the storm here, and I realized we were on the bay side of the house. A door opened on a bedroom, and moving about in that other room was a woman who looked broad and muscular enough for any emergency with Miss Johanna and her wheel chair.

The woman shut the door, and Miss Johanna and I were alone. She said,

"You look young. Helen Carrington did not mention age,

and I supposed— But youth is not a disadvantage here. I understand you have had no training as a nurse."

"None at all," I admitted.

She nodded with what seemed satisfaction.

"No doubt you've heard something of what your duties will be. There are three of us, my sister, my father, and myself. My father is past eighty, and perhaps the halest of the family. My sister is insane. I hope that fact has not been glossed over to you."

I said that it had not been.

"Insane, but not violent," Miss Johanna continued. "In fact, a stranger might suppose she was normal. The reason for this is that she has been properly restrained. Susan Mead, the last nurse, gave her a firm hand. I instructed Susan from the start as I expect to instruct you. I understand that you have done teaching—tutoring, that is. Any successful teacher is a disciplinarian. Leniency with my sister might be fatal. Once, when I was taking care of her—I have not always been disabled—she tried to jump out of a window. It was after that we put in the iron bars. A consistent, persistent firmness is the only possible attitude, and must be maintained from the start, so that in her disordered brain she will expect nothing. Do you know anything about mental illness?"

"A little," I said.

And that little, I might have told her, by experience. Had I not been mentally ill the night I groped about the garden? Could I not understand the torment of anyone who lived in the red twilight which was all I remembered of the hospital?

"Good," said Miss Johanna. "My father imagines he wants a companion for Zoé. A companion, when what she needs is a jailer. He knows nothing. The nurses we have had knew nothing. They merely supposed they knew."

Miss Johanna broke off to inquire,

"Are you by any chance a follower of Dr. Freud?"

I replied that I was not, that I had had no opportunity to study his theories.

Again the satisfied nod.

"I felt reasonably sure that a clergyman's daughter would not attempt to psychoanalyze her patient. They are likely, however, to pray, which is the reverse of the shield. I understand that your father was unorthodox, that he healed the sick by prayer. Many felt that he was cheapening the church. Would you undertake to heal by prayer?"

"I have not the faith or the understanding," I said. "We don't inherit those."

"And you are not here to pray," she added. "My sister's mind—her memory—must be left alone. She has been as she is for thirty years. She must not be disturbed. As I say, you are better without training or even experience. You must, however, be adamant in carrying out my instructions. Believe me, in spite of my affliction, I will know if those instructions are not obeyed."

I said nothing, certain that I would not be on Yonder long enough for instructions to matter. The miasma of the house had its source, I suspected, in the person of Johanna Croome. Bound to her chair, there diffused from her an immense and terrible energy, lashing against itself. She seemed to my tired eyes like a python in a cage, writhing, baneful. I remembered what Dane had said about wanting to hide from her eyes. They seemed to smolder, to burn, so that I wanted to close

43

my own and not look into them. I met them with what steadiness I could.

Did she hate all things—even the poor invalid—so much that my first lesson would be the discarding of compassion? True, I had been told, and by a nurse, that sympathy—compassion—was baggage a nurse disposed of independently. Illusions first, in that element of trays and bedpans, then sympathy. Otherwise, she would go mad. But why worry over parting with sympathy? I was not going to stay. Johanna Croome and I were enemies on sight.

Her voice came more quietly. "I don't wish to discourage you, Miss York. Tomorrow you will talk with my father and learn that the work here is light. The nurses have enjoyed the place, and none of them really wanted to leave. Now tell me about the Carringtons. Pony's marriage must have been a blow to her parents."

"It took her a long way off," I said. Apparently Miss Johanna didn't know that Pony's marriage was about over.

"And Dane's married, too," she said. "Is he as handsome as when he was a child? But you are too young to know. Helen wrote me that Pony grew into a quite pretty girl. Fritz I have never seen. He was born after they were here. Helen grew up on Point Muspa and here on Yonder. Now I suppose we are too dull for her, part of the stagnant backwater, while she is on the high seas, riding the crest."

The wheel chair creaked harshly.

"Thank you for coming down, Miss York." She could be gracious when she chose. "Please regard our interview as confidential. It will not be the last. Any time you find things difficult or troublesome I hope you will come to me."

44

I thanked her. The woman I had seen in the other room came out and opened the door for me. She wore a white uniform and a brown Dutch bob like a cap.

"This is Nannine," Miss Johanna said, and a smile lit the woman's broad, bland face, vanishing almost at once. "Breakfast is at nine," added Miss Johanna. "Is there anything you need?"

I mentioned a key to my door, having noticed that there was none.

"You will be in that room only tonight," said Miss Johanna coldly. "I doubt if the door has a key."

I went back to my room to find coffee in an ancient silver pot, and a plate of sandwiches. I had my bath, then sat in a flannel robe before the fire which had been renewed in my absence, and ate and drank. Afterward I tried to open one of the casement windows a crack, but the wind leaped in with such violence that I closed it again.

I climbed into bed, put out the light beside me, and amid the howling of the storm, went to sleep.

I hardly know what woke me, whether it was the opening and closing of the door, or the light that had come into the room. The light was no more than a candle. I lay watching the pointed flame and its nimbus, unable for a moment to distinguish more. Presently I saw that the candle was carried by a girl, and that she was bare-footed and bare-armed, clad only in a long thin nightgown. The candlelight ran down her hair which hung loose and blonde around her shoulders. She

45

moved across the room, not glancing at the bed, going straight to the closet, opening the door.

The closet was empty except for the hat and dress I had taken off. The girl set the candle on the bureau nearby. She pulled the dress from its hanger, examined it, laid it aside. She took down the hat, put it on and turned to the mirror, holding up the candle to study the effect. The hat did not please her and she returned it to the shelf. Again she examined the dress, then dropping it on a chair, drew the nightgown over her head and stood naked in the candle-light, a slim alabaster figure that might have escaped from a fountain.

Over her head went the dress. It was loose in the waist and without its belt dropped well below her knees. Smiling, satis-fied, she contemplated herself in the long mirror of the bath-room door. She spied my slippers and got into them, took the hat and put it on again, contemplated my coat spread over a chair, fingered its fur, rejected it.

Dressed in this strange fashion, her glance fell on an old breakfront bookcase, and she walked over to it, the loose slippers wobbling. She opened the desk compartment and her hands moved about inside it. There was a click and I realized that she had invaded some inner secret drawer. With a smile she took out what looked like a carved wooden box, closed the drawer, closed the desk.

Abruptly the door opened, and Nannine burst in.

"You wicked child," she said. "Come here at once."

The girl drew back against the wall, her eyes large in the candlelight. She laid down the box. Nannine strode over to her, snatched up the nightgown. "I'm sorry," she said to me as I sat up in bed watching them. "She was gone when I got back to her room."

"*This* is my room," said the girl, also looking at me, seeming to see me for the first time.

"Never mind," remarked Nannine, "those are not your clothes." She jerked off the hat, pulled the dress over the girl's head.

"Look at you now. Aren't you ashamed? Here, get into your nightgown."

The girl submitted as if with fatalism.

"Those shoes. Get out of those shoes."

The shoes were kicked deftly across the room, landing with a clatter. Nannine turned to me and the girl snatched up the box.

"Excuse all this," Nannine begged. "I thought she was asleep. Miss Johanna needed me. I can't be in two places at once. I hope it don't get you all waked up."

Nothing could do that, I assured her, and Nannine, seizing the candle and the girl's hand, went out and closed the door. I was alone again with the dark and the storm.

Who was the girl, I wondered, and what sort of place was this? I was uneasy now with my keyless door.

Yet even as I worried I fell asleep.

VI

I woke in the strange room and lay gazing at the sunlight pouring through the open shutters. I felt that it had been daylight a long time. In the stillness the clock on the mantel began to strike, eight chiming blows of a silver blacksmith's hammer on a bronze anvil.

A fire blazed on the hearth.

The girl had said that this room was hers—or had the girl been a dream? In any case, the clock looked as if it might belong to her. So did the painting above the mantel, a vivacious arrangement of birds and flowers. The clock was flanked by twin crystal vases. Those were like her, too.

Why had they given me her room?

I got out of bed and opened a window on the shining day, on a sea lying calm and deep blue, a white beach, and gulls flying in a cloudless sky. A child was playing on the beach, a small, fair-haired boy dressed in yellow swimming trunks. He waded in the fringe of blue water, ran along the sand, stopped to look up at the gulls, then while I watched him, he disappeared . . . Nowhere now. Standing still, looking up at the gulls—then gone.

Strange. He had looked like Dane.

Had the girl too been a ghost? No, there was my hat lying on the bureau where Nannine had left it. There were my slippers beside the hearth—she had retrieved them and placed them there. My dress in her agitation she had flung across a chair. The girl was not a ghost . . .

But the child had seemed even more real.

I looked down at the shrubs beneath my window, at the shell paths strewn with broken twigs and flowers. A vine climbed toward me bearing still its gold, goblet-shaped blossoms. At my right the stone façade rounded into a tower, and the vine crept over to embrace it, spreading on and up to where a window with iron bars across it looked out to sea.

The house seemed still asleep when I went downstairs. Blinds and curtains were drawn against the sun as they had been against the storm. The silence seemed fetid from having been shut in so long. I wandered from room to room. Surely some one would be awake, since it was close to nine o'clock.

The dark hangings I had noticed the night before were maroon-colored and of the finest brocade. Those in the immense parlors looked like antique velvet. Great Chinese vases sat on pedestals of carved teakwood, barbaric weapons hung on the walls. Cabinets held curios of jade, of cloisonné and ivory, and in one a small chest spilled curious rings and ornaments, including a gold chain and seal that might have been worn by a bishop.

The grand piano in the music room was locked. The harp,

leaning against it, was buttoned into its gray coat. All was dusted and in perfect order. All seemed to have been collected and placed there ages before.

The sound of a radio came to me and I went toward it, arriving at what appeared to be a den or smoking room. Here an old man sat sunk in an easy chair, listening to the news. He looked around as I came in, then rose with what was plainly an effort.

"Good morning, Miss York." A husky voice. "I am Judge Croome." A feeble pressure of my hand, a faint smile.

He looked like his daughter, Miss Johanna. The same black eyes and dominant nose. Perhaps under the white beard the same implacable mouth and chin. Unlike Miss Johanna, he gave the impression of being spent.

He indicated a chair, and the newscast over, asked if the storm had kept me awake, if my trip had been comfortable, if Richard had taken good care of me. He seemed hardly to hear my replies, but after each question lapsed into apparent abstraction, rousing himself, speaking again, hoarsely.

Richard Lowrie came in. He had been out and around the island to see what damage the storm had done. On the beach he had found a king conch shell, horny and rough, with a rose pink lining.

"Zoé collects shells," he said.

The breakfast chimes sounded and we went down the hall and into the long dining room. There were portraits on the walls and massive gold candlesticks and salvers on the great buffet. Miss Johanna sat in her place at the foot of the table. Her father introduced us, and remembering her injunction of the night before, I gave no sign that we had met.

Grapefruit, cereal, omelet and bacon. Small biscuits and aromatic coffee with heavy cream. Ezra waited on the table, moving noiselessly, an automaton.

Miss Johanna did most of the talking. The big baobab tree had blown down. "Odd," she said. "That tree has battled full-sized hurricanes for a hundred years. I wonder what it means. As for the lime trees, Hiram and his family had gathered the limes before the storm began, though I had not thought it would be necessary. The one tree they left—the bitter limes—was stripped by the wind. A freak squall."

Nannine appeared to help Miss Johanna into her wheel chair. Judge Croome asked me to come with him into his office. Richard said he would wait, and went out into the hall. It looked as if Miss Johanna would not be put into her chair until she and Nannine were alone. No . . . Ezra remained. I saw him advance to give aid as the judge and I stepped through one of the long French windows onto a veranda.

This was again the bay side of the house, shady at this hour, and cool. The judge indicated the garden beyond the step, a spread of bright tropical flowers, lifting their heads after the storm. There was a sundial at the center, and a stone bench under a large-leafed tree.

On the veranda he opened a door, signaling me with a slight gesture to precede him. He moved slowly, a stooped, rather heavy figure, leaning on a cane. When he sat down he gave the impression of becoming one with the chair. His black eyes, hooded like a hawk's, gazed at the floor. He looked like a melancholy bird brooding on its nest . . . He's as queer as the rest, Dane had said.

51

The book-lined office was in perfect order except for the enormous desk which was cluttered with letters and an assortment of legal-looking papers. No doubt he had given orders that the desk was not to be disturbed. He had motioned me to a small carved love seat beneath the portrait of a lady. Both portrait and love seat seemed out of place in the room.

"I no longer go to my office on the mainland," he explained, lifting his eyelids, looking at me. "This place is adequate for the little work I do now, most of it in connection with Yonder. We farm the key. Johanna directs the work. Richard is a great help to her when he's here, since she can't get out now among the men. Richard's father was our family physician. He died some time ago. Richard was finally alone, so he joined us here on Yonder. A link between us and the world. In a wide sense, I mean. Richard's an explorer, a first-rate adventurer. You may know his books. Has his own place on the key, a short walk away."

Richard Lowrie. Certain collateral reading at St. Hilda's came back to me. I was sure that had been the name . . .

The judge appeared not to expect an answer. He had his daughter's gift of monologue, and I was to learn that an answer, even to what seemed a direct question, was apt to throw him off the track. He sat for a moment in heavy-lidded abstraction, then spoke to me as Miss Johanna had done—yet differently—about the work I was to do.

"It has always seemed to me," he said, "that Zoé's nurses have been too clinical. One of them—perhaps the most highly trained—wrote a history of the case, as far as she knew it, and the account was published in a medical journal. The first I knew of it was when physicians from other parts began to arrive on Yonder, asking to see my daughter. The situation was intolerable. Of course I dismissed the nurse, but it was some time before the repercussions of that article died down.

"Susan Mead, the last nurse—who died quite suddenly—was thoroughly dependable, a methodical, easy-going person, what is known as a practical nurse. She had common sense. Perhaps it was unreasonable of me to wish that she should also have imagination. I would prefer that you do not think of Zoé as ill or deranged, that you forget anything you may have heard about her, and accept her as you find her.

"My niece, Helen Carrington, writes me that you are not medically trained. That may be an advantage. It may help you to consider Zoé as a companion, let us say a playmate, rather than a patient—to be her friend, rather than a nurse. Is that possible?"

"It will be easier," I said.

"Mmmm . . ." slightly taken aback. "I hoped so. We have never crossed her when it could be helped. She takes her walks on the beach like anyone else, though of course not alone. Sometimes she has to be made to come in, but that is natural. One morning a week she visits with me a little while, then goes in to see her sister, though she always objects to that, has to be coaxed or bribed, has delusions that Johanna would like to kill her. It is one of her few symptoms of derangement, the illusion that she is persecuted. It can only be ignored. Johanna would feel hurt if Zoé slighted her. Neither Johanna nor I can climb the stairs. Johanna has had arthritis for ten years now, and I am nearly eighty-four. Zoé is in her own world upstairs. It is better so.

"You may leave her with me when you feel the need of

going for a walk alone. Every Wednesday, from one to six in the afternoon, Nannine Finkel, the housekeeper, will relieve you. On Sundays, if you wish to go over to the mainland to church, there is the *Blade,* Richard's launch. Richard or Nannine will take you. The nurses have always gone. Zoé stays with me. We walk in the garden. You see it is almost as if she were free." He sank into his thoughts, emerged and added, "I hope you will like it on Yonder."

I said that I hoped so, too, yet I had not lost the feeling that I would soon be gone. Daylight had not dissipated the miasma of that house. I felt it even in the judge's office with its window open on the bright garden where he would walk with Zoé when I felt the need of being alone. This office would be near Miss Johanna's room. It was in the same wing, apparently looked out on the same veranda.

The judge's tired eyes met mine.

"I want you," he said, "to come to me with any problem, any suggestion. My daughter's wardrobe now. As a young girl she seemed to me frivolous, extravagant. It may be I did not understand her, for Johanna was always sensible. I regret that I ever objected to the finery Zoé bought, ever made an issue of the bills. I did this seldom, but there were times . . ."

He brooded. Then, "I have told the nurses that when they saw a dress or any other thing that might please or amuse her they were to buy it. I say the same to you. Notice the shop windows when you go into Muspa. We have accounts, of course, at all the stores . . . Incidentally, she does not know that Susan Mead is dead. She was very fond of Susan, and I think it best not to tell her. That is all, Miss York, unless there is some question you would like to ask me."

54

There was none, the matter of salary having been settled by mail. He rose. Slowly he crossed the room, opened an inside door. We went along the stone passage I had traveled the night before with Ezra, arriving in the front hall where Richard Lowrie met us. Richard and I went up the stair to the second floor, then climbed a longer, steeper flight. He knocked on a door and Nannine opened it. We entered a tower room, large and bright and perfectly round. White curtains stirred in the breeze from the barred windows. A small table was set for breakfast.

Nannine indicated the bed, a great ornamented testered thing like something out of Spanish legend. In it, my visitor of the night before lay asleep, her shining hair spread over the pillow.

"She saw your light out the window last night," Nannine explained to me. "It got her excited and she didn't sleep much. But then she's always wild when the wind blows."

The sleeper stirred. She stretched round white arms and sat up, shaking back her hair. She was a child, fresh and beautiful as the morning. She could not have been over twenty.

"Richard!" she cried, and he went over to her and gave her the shell. She held it to her ear, listening, smiling, then reaching up, shared its music with him.

"Sound as a bell," he said.

She slid from the bed, still holding the shell, and Nannine brought a Chinese kimono and put it on her.

"This is the day," she said, pushing back the gay, embroidered sleeves. She flew to the window and looked out on ocean and sky and wheeling gulls. "The day!" she cried, turning about.

"So it is," said Richard. "And now I want you to meet some one who has come a long way to see you. Her name is Olive. Olive, this is Zoé."

I smiled and said her name. She came slowly and held the shell to my ear, her green-blue eyes meeting mine.

"Susan's dead," she said.

Richard and Nannine glanced at each other.

"You thought I didn't know," remarked Zoé. "I know everything. I hear, too. I hear the earth turning around. I hear people thinking."

She warmed to our attention.

"The gulls talk to me," she said. "They tell me things. Only this was not a gull, the one that came in last night. It was white like a gull, but its mantle was gray, and it wore a black cap because it brought bad news. Its name was Wanda. Do you know what it was?" turning to me. "It was a tern. Nannine drove it out with the hearthbroom."

"She dreams things. She doesn't know the dream from the real."

Nannine spoke as if Zoé were not present, or as if she were inanimate.

Richard said, "Olive is a stranger, Zoé. You must be good to her, make her want to stay."

Zoé gazed at me. I had never seen such eyes, mermaid's eyes, sea-green, sea-blue. She said nothing.

Richard went to the door. He was leaving, and I wanted to talk with him, to ask him a hundred things.

"I'll see you again," he said to me, and was gone.

56

My link with the world, as Judge Croome had said. My link with reality. Yet strangely enough in this lofty room, with the sunlit Zoé, I seemed to have ascended out of the fogs and mist of the house into the open sky, into another world.

VII

Nannine came out of the bathroom, closing the door.

"I've got her in the tub," she said. "Maybe that'll hold her for a while. You and the tern, both at once. I told her a tern couldn't get through those bars. You know what she said to me? 'You're not very bright, Nannine.' *She* said *that*. I hope the judge won't think I told her about Susan Mead. You never know what she'll come up with."

Nannine turned away, beginning to speak rapidly, having seen in my face perhaps the question I had wanted to ask Richard Lowrie.

"This is your room, Miss York, just next—two steps down. Part of the main house. I've unpacked your things. The dresses are in the closet there, your blouses and lingerie in the bureau drawers. All your little jars and bottles in the bathroom cabinet."

"Thank you, Nannine."

"I envy you your dresses and being able to wear what you please on your job, the nicer the better, because Zoé likes pretty things, and the judge feels she mustn't be depressed

58

or know she's got a nurse. They call me a housekeeper, and so I am, but I'm primarily Miss Johanna's nurse, and she likes me in uniform. I prefer mufti, and I used to have long hair and do it in waves, but on this job I chop it off, which I did even before bobs were stylish—just to save time. As for Susan, she liked her uniform but they made her lay it by, like I say, because of Zoé. She was a good nurse and knew almost as much as a doctor, but it's nice to have someone with a pleasant voice. Susan's voice was raucous, though she wasn't raucous herself. I hope you stay. I'm sure Miss Johanna hopes so, too, though you'd never get her to say so."

"Nannine," I said, "how old is Zoé?"

She opened a drawer in the highboy and began to lay out Zoé's lavishly trimmed underclothes.

"I can't say, Miss York." A half-mumble, a glance at the bathroom door as if afraid I had been overheard.

"As old as Miss Johanna?"

"Not quite, I think."

"She looks much younger. Young enough to be her child." Nannine opened the ponderous old wardrobe.

"Maybe she does. I see her every day, and I'm used to her. I want you to notice how she acts about her clothes, and with no reason. This pink shantung, for instance, good as money can buy. Susan got it for her in Miami, paid a lot for it. Watch when Zoé sees I've laid it out."

"Have you been here long, Nannine?"

"Nine years. Nearly ten."

"Zoé must have been a child when you came."

"Well, she was certainly spoiled like a child, and she is yet. Her first nurse was to blame for that. She was an old Negro woman named Belen, and she'd been with Judge and Mrs. Croome from the time they married, nursed both Miss Johanna and Zoé. Belen got too old for the stairs."

"Judge Croome said that about himself. If there were an elevator . . ."

"They'll never have one. They live just like in the old days. You can't tell 'em anything. The old man's stubborn as a mule, and Miss Johanna . . ."

Nannine stopped abruptly. Her face as she looked at me became fixed, and I thought she turned pale. She rose and opened the door, though no one had knocked. Ezra stood outside.

"Miss Johanna wants you," he said in his low, level voice. How long had he been there, standing so close with only the door between us? His face betrayed nothing.

"All right," Nannine replied.

She closed the door and took from the pocket of her uniform a pair of keys on a ring. One was a huge thing like the key to an ancient city. It unlocked the tower room, she said. The other smaller key belonged to my own room.

"Carry them about with you," she admonished. "And keep the doors locked. That was the trouble last night. I'll call down for her breakfast, have Cook send it up. I hope you won't mind the wooden cutlery. The silver was taken away from her a long time ago. And you're to keep your scissors and nail files locked up . . . I'll show you where the dumb-waiter is."

It was just outside the door. Nannine opened it, called in a shrill voice down the shaft. She seemed nervous since the appearance of Ezra.

Zoé was out of the tub and had begun to dress, sitting naked on the floor, pulling on sheer silk stockings and fragile slippers, getting into the elaborate slip and panties Nannine had laid out. She wore no girdle nor bra, her slenderness, her high small breasts not requiring them. I buttoned the pink dress with its silver belt encircling her hips. After the mode of the moment it came just to her knees. Her legs were beautiful, like Pony's. She took from her bureau a small crystal ball hanging from a jeweled bow-knot, pinned it carefully on her dress. I saw that it was a watch—a bull's-eye. Through its clear glass you could see all the fairy-like machinery.

Nannine returned after her session with the dumb-waiter.

"Breakfast will be right up. I won't be gone long. Judge Croome said I'm to go with you on your walk, this first time."

At the whistle of the dumb-waiter I brought in the breakfast, keeping an eye on the door lest the prisoner fly out. Zoé, however, had gone over to her shells. She kept them in a glass cabinet and was trying to fit the conch into their careful arrangement. She took her place at the table and I sat down opposite, pouring her coffee.

"Aren't you hungry?" she asked.

I explained that I had had breakfast. "But I'll eat lunch with you, and dinner."

"Don't bother," drinking her papaya juice. "I like to eat alone. I'm going to take my walk alone, too. This is the day."

"But I want you to show me the beach."

"The beach is there. You can see it for yourself. Besides, I'm going on the bay side. Johanna doesn't know. No one knows."

"*I* know, because you've told me."

She laid down the wooden spoon she had picked up.

"Do you know why they make me wear these clothes?" she demanded. "I'll tell you. It's because they hate me."

"No one hates you, Zoé. Besides, your clothes are beautiful."

"They are not mine," she answered. "And they are funny. This dress now. They make me wear it to fool someone. They want me to dress so that he won't know me. He'll think I'm somebody else in this funny dress. I'll show them. I'll wave and call," waving the spoon, "and he'll know me anyhow. Soon's I see the boat, soon's I see him looking for me. If I'm not on the bay side, he looks on the beach . . . They want him not to find me."

She stirred her coffee.

"Your clothes are funny, too," she said thoughtfully. "As for me, I have decent things if I could find them. Johanna is at the bottom of all this."

Someone knocked, and I opened the door. A young colored girl came in. She brought a mop and a carton of cleanser. Her hair was in oiled braids pinned with blue celluloid bows. She smiled a greeting and began to make the bed.

"Stella, too," said Zoé. "Stella hides my clothes."

"Your clothes are right here, Miss Zoé."

"You hear her?" cried Zoé, rising from the table. She unfastened the bull's-eye watch and laid it on the bureau, unfastened the silver belt, then abruptly tore off her pink dress and was about to stamp on it when Stella and I rescued it. She sprang to the wardrobe, snatching out its contents, flinging them about, Stella gathering them up, restoring them, placidly, as if it all went with cleaning the room.

62

"I hate you," Zoé said to me. "You, too, you thief," turning on Stella. "You're all thieves. You're all robbers and devils. I hate you all."

She sat down again, burying her head in her arms, sobbing aloud.

We walked along the beach, Nannine, Zoé and I.

Here was the ocean, the vast Atlantic, that I had longed to see. I gave my heart to its thunder, to its clean salt smell and bright blue flying wind.

This was the beach where I had seen the child, running, watching the gulls. Now it was Zoé I saw, flying ahead of me, the sandpipers scattering before her. Her mood was gay, though she had pled for the bay side instead of the beach. Too far, Nannine had answered, and too spongy after the rain.

Always, Nannine explained, she must find some excuse for not going to the bay side. The real reason was that the place was infested with rocks and caves, so that Zoé became more of a chore to watch.

"Always getting herself wet, even here," she added. "There'll come times when you'll wonder anybody like her should be allowed outdoors. Then you'll remind yourself she's not violent or dangerous, but she would be if you locked her up. Not dangerous, just a nuisance."

What a world it was! Helen Carrington had said there would be rainbow water. It was true. Only in the shallows at the edges of Key West have I seen that olive and violet, lime-green and blue. Shells strewed the beach, washed up by the storm. Here was a pink tellen, Nannine cried, a shell small as a thumbnail. "Zoé!" she called. "Here's a tellen."

Zoé seemed not to hear as she skimmed along. Nannine had coaxed her back into the pink dress, along with a sailcloth jacket and beach sandals. Nannine dropped the shell into her own pocket.

We came to a cabaña with two beach chairs beside it.

"All right, Zoé."

Zoé flew away from us, following the white crescent of the beach. There was a pier with a clump of palms nearby. Zoé stopped under the palms. Slim and straight as a figure on the prow of a ship, she stood looking out to sea. After a time she sat down on a reef shaded by the palms, still watching the sea.

"She's forgotten us," Nannine said.

From our beach chairs I could look back at the house, a sprawling medieval pile with towers and turrets, a stone wall around it and an iron gate.

"Is there a dungeon?" I asked Nannine.

"I don't know," she said gravely. "There's a chapel, if you know how to find it. The judge was a good churchman, they say, while his wife was alive. But this chapel . . . The Croomes away back must have been strange people."

"Strange?"

"Well, they were great travelers, and they brought things back. They didn't really want a chapel, I guess, but all the old castles had them, so they put it there. You couldn't use it for a wedding or a funeral, it's too tucked away. I wouldn't hunt it up, if I were you. And there's a ballroom too, right on your floor. Built for a banqueting hall. When the storms are bad you can hear sounds coming out of it, men carousing, drinking and laughing, like what you call a wassail. I hope you're not afraid of ghosts."

I said that I had never seen one. And yet—the child. That morning . . . But the girl had not been a ghost, so perhaps the child . . . Yet he had vanished while I looked at him.

Nannine was watching Zoé.

She seemed a simple person, Nannine, yet in the house she had been adroit in evading my questions.

It was odd that no one cared to tell me the history of Zoé's case. Helen Carrington had begun to speak of it, then had fallen silent, a veil dropping over her face. Apparently the members of the Croome household had always been reticent, even to the point of seeking no cure for the ailing girl. The strange doctors they had sent away.

I, too, looked at Zoé, waiting beneath her palm tree.

"Why did she say, 'This is the day'?" I asked.

"She always says that. She'll say it tomorrow."

"But why?"

"You can't account for what even normal people say. What worries me is she ought to be walking, taking exercise. Mr. Lowrie's the only one can get her to do it. He has a place down at the end of the key. Writes books about islands and all he sees when he's away on his yawl. Did you ever see a boat equipped to be sailed across the ocean by one man? Well, you will when he sets out again."

Nannine stood up.

"You have to keep an eye on Zoé, have to watch in case she gets a notion to go into the water just like she is. I can't swim, can you?"

"Not enough to rescue anyone. Hasn't she a bathing suit?"

"She won't wear it. Says it's indecent. But she'd as soon go in in nothing at all as not. She's like a baby that way. Like I say, you can't look for consistency."

"Zoé seems unhappy about her clothes," I said when Nannine had sat down again.

"I know. And they get her the best. It's a waste of money."

"Why don't they find the others, the ones she talks about?"

Nannine shook her head.

"She don't know what she's saying. She'd tear those up, too."

"But the ones she remembers—before she was taken ill."

"Thirty years ago? Who could find those?"

"Is there an attic?"

"Oh, yes. The stair's on your floor, at the end of the north passage. I'm surprised Miss Johanna hasn't made a bonfire of the junk up there. She likes to burn things, old things especially. I don't think she would have saved any of Zoé's clothes."

"Still," I said, "we might look for them. If they would make her happy."

"Yes, if they would. But I don't know when I could get at it. I haven't enough help in this place. Just Stella to do the cleaning, and Ezra to wait table and help with Miss Johanna —and the cook. Four people to keep a house this size. The mold and rust are something awful to contend with, and the moths get into clothes and carpets and hangings. They don't have carpets and hangings down here these days. That is, nobody else does . . . And the mildew. The mildew's terrible."

"But not much dust," I said.

"No, not much dust. But if there's any at all Miss Johanna sees it. She makes tours of the lower floor in her wheel chair, and if anything's out of place, I hear about it. Upstairs Ezra snoops around to spot a bit of lint or a broken shutter to report. Lucky for me, most of the place is shut up, but the way they want the rest of it kept you'd think they were expecting company, though they never are." She grew thoughtful. "Even if we found Zoé's clothes, they'd be all out of style."

"That's what she wants," I said. "That's what she remembers."

"It might be. But Miss Johanna would— Well, once when I was cleaning out a closet I found a doll. I brought it upstairs and Zoé grabbed it, said it was hers. She rocked it and sang to it and began to ask for a blue china cradle I didn't know anything about. Miss Johanna found out and said the doll was making Zoé worse, rousing dormant memories was what she said, and she burned it in her fireplace right before Zoé's eyes. Zoé jumped on her, of course, scratching and screaming. All I could do to pull her off."

"No wonder Zoé doesn't want to call on Miss Johanna," I said.

"Well . . . Susan almost had to push her in sometimes. But it's part of the treatment. Miss Johanna thinks she knows more about insanity than anybody else. And she does read about it, study about it, in all sorts of books. Books on magic and hypnotism . . . But Zoé's not really—I've worked with insane people. Zoé's different. Keeps herself tidy. Bathes. Buffs her nails, brushes her hair. She's like somebody in a dream. *We* dream when we're asleep, don't we?

"She does go crazy if they keep her shut up. And she does get upset about her clothes. But long as she gets her walks and can sit on the beach or the bay side like she's doing now things go along pretty smooth. Miss Johanna's against the walks, says Zoé'll drown herself yet, but the judge won't listen to her . . . Old Belen never would let Zoé go in to see Miss Johanna. Even Judge Croome couldn't make her. But Belen couldn't stop Miss Johanna from going to see Zoé. Now, of course, the arthritis keeps Miss Johanna down. But she got rid of Belen. Persuaded the judge she was too old."

"Where's Belen now?"

"In Muspa. Got her own little house. Gets around better than most people her age. It went hard with Belen when she had to go. Made me kind of sick that day, with Zoé not knowing she was leaving for good, telling her what to bring back, and Belen keeping her face turned away so Zoé wouldn't see she was crying.

"Miss Johanna can do anything with her father, give her time. Finally they got hold of Susan. Judge told Susan what he wanted her to do, but it was Miss Johanna trained her, or thought she did. Susan didn't believe that irritating and frightening Zoé—forms of the shock treatment, Miss Johanna said—was the right way. She was good to Zoé when they were alone. Sometimes I think—"

Nannine stopped. I had been listening hopefully, remembering what Dane had said, "People tell you more than they intend. You listen, and they talk too much." It was not curiosity alone. I felt in a vague way that I could be of more help to Zoé if I knew the root of her trouble.

Nannine said as if answering this thought,

"You might talk to Mr. Lowrie. He does more for Zoé than anybody. Got her interested in the shells, brings them to her from everywhere. Takes her fishing. Susan liked to go with them, so did the other nurses. I went once—over to Lonely Key. Nothing would do that day on Lonely but Zoé must go back into the jungle. I thought she *had* to go, but no, she was just hunting something, hunting a house or something. What we found was a diamond-back rattler. I screamed till Mr. Lowrie came and killed it with his machete. Zoé never uttered a sound, just looked at the snake and watched him cut its head off. He said the breed was *adamanteus,* the biggest of the diamond-backs. Picked it up with a stick and stretched it out, six feet long. I'll never forget walking along that sort-of-path in the jungle and seeing that thing coiled and rearing up its head in front of us. Zoé wanted its rattles, and he cut them off and gave them to her. I don't know what she ever did with them. I hope I never run across them.

"He bought her a battery radio, Mr. Lowrie did, and a record player with some old-time records Miss Johanna would have thrown out if she knew about them. I wouldn't tell her and Susan wouldn't, and Ezra don't know they *are* old-time. I sometimes think . . ."

That phrase again. Nannine amended it. "I honestly believe Miss Johanna don't want to dig up what's in Zoé's mind. I believe she's afraid of it. She don't want Zoé to get well and remember."

"Remember what?"

Nannine looked away, squinting against the sun.

"Susan asked me that when she first came, said she needed to know. I couldn't tell her because I didn't know myself.

Nobody knows except the family, and that includes Ezra, I guess, and Belen. They don't talk. And I think they don't any of them—even Belen—want Zoé to get well."

"It's strange she stays so young," I said.

"In looks, you mean. But she's young in every way, and like a girl. She hasn't aged a day since I came. You'll never know Ezra," Nannine broke off to add. "He's part Indian. Not Seminole, that other. Calusa. His grandfather ate powdered glass and died rather than go live in the swamps like the other Florida Indians when our government took over. Miss Johanna swears by Ezra. He can help her in and out of her chair better than anybody. Looks like he reads her mind."

The sun had become almost too warm. Nannine rose, and we walked along the beach to Zoé's clump of palms. Zoé had risen and was standing at the tide line in the rainbow shallows. Nannine put an arm around her.

"Time to go in now."

Zoé looked at her as if she had never seen her before.

"Time for lunch," said Nannine. "We'll come back to-morrow."

"Tomorrow," repeated Zoé, and looked again at the sea.

Suddenly she twisted and was gone, was wading into the water. Nannine waded after, grabbed her.

"Look at you now, all wet," towing her onto the beach. "And you wanted to wear your good shoes, remember?"

Zoé made no answer. Gazing before her like a sleepwalker, she trailed with us back to the house.

VIII

To think that every day she went through the same round. Every day the same hope, the same frustration. Who was it she had waited under the palm tree to see on this, the day? He had not come and she had walked into the sea. "She's always getting herself wet," Nannine had said.

Had Nannine attached no significance to that walk into the sea? Would Zoé sometime elude her watchers and end this vigil by drowning herself? How could the human heart endure this perpetual alternation of joy and defeat?

Apparently it left no more trace than the waves left on the sand. By evening Zoé had forgotten, was showing me her shells, the pink tellen, the jingle shell, the lion's paw.

"Susan found this one before she went away and died. Richard brought me this from Africa. I found this rose cockle myself. I can hear the sea in even the little ones. One night I saw an octopus come out of the water and walk along the beach on its toes—on its hands—like a toe dancer. It was moonlight. Papa saw it too. I was a child. We got out of its way."

I knew that the fantastic tale was true. From the start I could tell when Zoé dealt with fact and when with dreams.

At the sound of the dumb-waiter she rose and set the table. Yellow dishes and a bowl of lavender flowers that she said came from the bauhenia tree; delicate embroidered linen, and wooden spoons.

"The doilies are out of my hope chest, there in the corner. It's carved cedrella wood, and came from Bali."

We ate our lunch of shrimp pilau and wild rice, with a pineapple salad served in half a papaya.

"I told Nannine things must be nice for you. I want you to stay. I want you to stay until you die, like Susan."

We played euchre. She taught me with some impatience, for I played nothing but bridge, and that without distinction. She read to me from du Maurier's *Trilby*, both of us curled in the window seat with the phonograph going. She cared very little for the small battery radio, said that I might keep it in my room. The phonograph played ragtime and waltzes that I had never heard, records Richard Lowrie had brought her.

"Let's dance, Olive."

She laid down the book, and I put my arm around her, though when we girls danced with each other at school it was always someone else who led. She was light and yielding as a reed, but her steps did not mate with mine—I couldn't waltz like that—and after a few turns she drew away and danced alone, or with some unseen companion. She dipped and twirled, tiptoeing now and then—like the octopus, she said—her white arms extended, her bright hair falling back.

That night she said to me, "I'm going to get well."

"But you're not sick, Zoé."

She gazed at me with strange tormented eyes, sitting up in bed, leaned closer, took my hand.

"Something's wrong," she said. "I can't find out what it is. Sometimes I chase it through the dark. I fly on wings through miles of dark. I almost catch it, then it goes through a door, and a hand comes out and shuts the door."

She lay back on the pillows, still holding to my hand.

"You're coming with me after this. You're going to go ahead and shut the door before it goes through, and you'll wait there for me. You're not afraid, are you? You'll stay."

One window in my room opened on the sea. I stood before it a long time that night, after Zoé had fallen asleep, stood looking at the waves, listening to their all-pervading sound. To live on Yonder was like living in a shell, Helen Carrington had said. It was true. Like living in a shell, closed inside its murmur, deaf to the echoes of the world. Forgetting. In time.

A full moon floated close to the horizon, making a path across the water. In its light a child trudged along the beach, carrying his pail and sand shovel. Out so late, I thought, with octopuses and heaven knew what abroad.

The child vanished, and I knew.

I could not forget Dane in this place. I had buried him a thousand miles away, yet he would always haunt the beach of Yonder. I must leave. I must go to the ends of the earth.

But I had promised Zoé I would stay.

On my afternoon off Richard Lowrie took me for a stroll. Yonder was a coral island with patches of marl and leaf mold

73

and rich black muck. I saw pineapples growing, and limes and sapodillas, papaya trees, slim and unbranched, spreading an umbrella of leaves above their orange-gold fruit; sugar apples and tamarinds, and melons misshapen from lying among the rocks. I saw men set banana roots in baskets of earth and lower them into rock holes that had been made with a crowbar.

Small green pumpkins climbed trees and hung like fruit. Prickly pears and prickly apples flourished in rocky patches flooded with sea water. There were no orchard rows. Everything grew in knots and clusters as if they were wild. In a dark-leafed hollow what looked like many white flowers turned out to be a flock of snowy egrets, resting in the cool. The place was full of swamp smell, as if no air reached it.

We walked through the hollow to the bay. Here were limestone and coral rocks, a boathouse and a pier with a small launch tied, and a mangrove fence crawling out into the sea, a shield, Richard Lowrie said, against heavy seas and the flotsam of storms.

This was the side that Zoé had begged to visit on her outing. It was only a short walk, for the island narrowed here, but Nannine had told her it was too far, and I had said on the first morning I took her out alone, "I don't know the way."

"I will show you," she had answered, and I had been forced to find other excuses. The bay side looked harmless enough, and Zoé had not been venturesome with me. Some day I would let her guide me here.

We passed an old kitchen midden, relic of the Indians, made of dirt dragged from the bay bottom and mixed with bones and broken pots. Banana melons covered it now, and glossy red tomatoes. Asparagus grew wild, the cauliflowers had two heads, and potatoes were so abundant that key farmers welcomed the inroads of raccoons.

Again we were in the hollow where the egrets had been. Richard Lowrie called it the grove. It seemed darker with the white birds gone, and the swamp smell seemed heavier. The grove was an eerie place, sinister with its snakelike vines and their drooping blood-red flowers, with the naked roots of trees rising from the ground to trip you. Richard Lowrie said that nothing would grow in the hollow, nothing you planted.

"It seemed to me that mushrooms might thrive here," he said. "They didn't, though the poisonous toadstools flourish."

He took my arm, guiding me among the roots. We were not following the path we had taken before.

"My house is in there," he said, and I saw a low green roof through the trees. We left the grove and came out into the sunlight on what he said was Pirate's Finger, a slender peninsula, pointing into the Atlantic.

"This is where Captain Kidd hung his false beacons," Richard Lowrie said. "Yonder Key was their hideout, and wrecking was their business. We might find a chest of emeralds if we dug for it, or pieces of eight."

"Unless the Indians got them," I said.

"No, the Indians were gone by then. They called the island Chassahowitska, by the way. The pirates couldn't say it, and spoke of it as Yonder Key. Would it surprise you to hear that the first Croome on Yonder—the judge's great-grandfather— was a pirate?"

I thought of Miss Johanna, and said no.

"He came back when things had quieted down and made

75

his home here. His cronies used to visit him—those that hadn't been hanged—and they had big feasts in the old banquet hall. His wife wouldn't have the racket downstairs, or the cronies either—or so the tale goes. I've never known whether he was granted the key, or bought it. Anyhow, he built this house, replica of a castle in Cornwall he'd admired as a boy."

"It looks as if it had grown there."

"It does. Old Jared Croome built a good house. Coquina rock from Cuba, mahogany from Honduras. Got the lime by burning conch shells. Other generations have added the bathrooms, but Jared welded his house to the island itself. A breakwater protects it from the sea, a breakwater built by the polyp. So far, it has laughed at hurricanes."

I looked back at the castle fortress, thought of its robust builder and the strange brood it housed today. The melancholy old man, the woman twisting in her chains of hate, the frantic golden bird high in the tower. I thought of the treasures in the great drawing room, the priceless salvers and candlesticks on the buffet. There were no riches under our feet, I suspected, except the soil itself and the wells of pure fresh water that my guide told me rose and fell with the tides. Jared Croome, before he died, had unearthed his loot. Even so, he left little money, Richard Lowrie said. It was the judge's father who had enriched the family—with a fleet of windjammers carrying rum and molasses from the West Indies. Sold his boats finally to Uncle Sam for a king's ransom.

We sat under an old banyan tree far out where the false beacons had once hung. Around us blowing waves of pink grass flowed down to the water's edge. I could see the light-house on Beacon Key, gray against the blazing sapphire sky. In a shallow inlet a lonely blue heron stood on one leg and slept. ("Yes." Dane's voice. "That was where I saw the herons dance.")

I said to Richard Lowrie, "I've read your *Tonga*. It was in the school library."

"Required reading," he surmised.

"But I read it twice. It made me love the sea before I'd seen anything bigger than a lake."

He nodded, sitting with his elbows on his knees. I noticed his hands, finely shaped, yet capable looking, tanned like his face, a face at once remote and friendly, rugged yet intellectual, full of contradictions, or perhaps of contrasts. I wondered if anyone ever got to know him, or if he showed them one side only. He was young, I thought, to have that single line between his brows, a line so heavily indented that it remained even when humor came into his eyes.

We were talking about the sea, and how it was inherent in us to love it, seeing we had emerged from it, or so we were told, and carried its salt in our veins.

Then presently he spoke of Zoé and her strange perennial youth.

"She's locked in one moment," he said. "Time for her has stopped. She knows nothing about it, and so she grows no older."

"How is that possible?" I asked, but faintly, knowing that Father would have believed.

"It's happened before," Richard Lowrie answered. "There's a well-known, well-substantiated case in England of a woman whose age was checked, as Zoé's was, by shock. She was seventy-four when she died, and looked like a young girl. There have been other instances, not on record. Zoé's case will not be chronicled if her family have their way."

"But time goes on," I said, "in spite of her not knowing it."

"Are you sure?" he asked. "Isn't time a matter of records? We couldn't grasp eternity, so we invented time. Clocks and calendars. Days of the week, of the month. Years, centuries. The planets—our planet—influencing us, changing us, by revolving around the sun."

"Sounds like astrology."

"It does, of course. At any rate, that's what makes time—records. And if there were no time, there'd be no age. We never think of eternity as making us older, and we could live in eternity now if we wanted to. The return of spring would be merely the return of a friend, not another milestone. That's all eternity is, the absence of time."

"But we grow up. We don't remain children. Surely that's time, too."

"No. An individual appears, develops, is revealed finally as a man, a woman. Then we say decay sets in, age, death. That's time. Development is the law of life. It's not a part of development to be destroyed."

"And you think we could divorce ourselves from time just as Zoé . . ."

"Better than Zoé, because we would do it intelligently. You might say Zoé is a captive, imprisoned in a moment. She merely proves something—that time is mental, that a single human being can remain outside its influence."

"I know that time is mental," I said. "I know that you can

78

age in a month of grief or worry, that a day can be years long, and that other days can pass like nothing."

"And the length of a day," he answered, "changes as we grow older. Days are long when you're a kid, then they shorten, and pretty soon, when we reach what we call the meridian, we hurry like a horse when he heads for home."

"How can we do without clocks?" I wondered.

He smiled his slow smile. "I'm afraid we can't. But they needn't be a part of the general hypnotism. We begin as soon as a child is born. He's one hour old, we say. *Old.* A newborn child. He's a month old. A year old. We keep that up till he takes hold himself, picks up the mesmeric count. Pretty soon he's old, and no kidding."

"I'd say Zoé was eighteen, if I didn't know."

"Zoé was older than that—twenty-one, to be exact. It happened thirty years ago. To me, too, she looks eighteen. I never think of her as anything else. I doubt if anyone does. And she thinks of herself as young. Time doesn't touch her within or without. And her eyes don't observe change. Her father, her sister, even inanimate objects, are just as they were the day she was struck by whatever bolt it was. She may remember in a way what happened yesterday or last year, but always today is the day. She never moves past it. If time is man's invention—and I believe it is—man can control it. I could do it. You could do it."

"It would take too much vigilance." I had almost said it would take too much time. "I'd rather just go on, grow past things."

Yet he had said that it was the law of life to grow, though not to grow old. Still, I thought, watching the blue heron who had not moved, why should anyone prolong youth? I said aloud a line of a half-forgotten poem, " 'Time is a kind friend, he will make us old.' "

Again that slow smile. "We love our inventions. We hate to make war on them. Don't want to bother. We'd like to stay young, but only by finding some Land of Heart's Desire or drinking of a Fountain of Youth, confusing it with magic. But Zoé, now—"

He paused, and I asked, wondering if he would evade me, "Was it shock?"

"Yes," he said. "My father was her physician, and he said that she was violent for a year, then settled into this. He said that it was not amnesia."

"Did he tell you what it was?"

"Vaguely. I never asked him, never thought about it then. Perhaps he really didn't know. Anyhow, it all happened before I was born. When I was a kid I used to come with him on his visits to Yonder. I liked it better than any other place. Later I was away a lot—at school, in the Navy. Something always pulled me back here. Finally, the judge asked me to come and live on Yonder, deeded me a piece of land at the tip of the key, told me to build me a house there—a gift from him, and at a time when I was without a home, or any ties at all."

"And the family have never—" I was still thinking of Zoé.

"Never a word. I remember my father said once that Johanna had been as handsome a girl as he ever saw, and the judge a fine figure of a man, gallant and fiery (which I can believe) and eloquent; made friends easily, and had been expected to run for the Senate. When it came to Zoé, all my old man said was that shock had caused her illness, and that shock might cure her."

"Then no one knows."

"There's gossip enough in the village, some of it rather gruesome. But, as you say, no one knows—outside the family."

"And the family includes Ezra," I said. "And old Belen."

I rose, knowing it was time for me to get back. I looked again at the blowing natal grass, at the heron standing so still he scarcely seemed alive.

"I wouldn't ask Ezra if I were you," Richard Lowrie said.

We took the beach road under a flame and green sunset.

IX

Nannine had said the attic stair was on our floor, at the end of the north passage. Investigating, I could find no stair until I opened a door. There it was, steep and dark, smelling of dampness and mold. That night I took a lamp—there was no electricity above the second floor—and went up to the attic in search of Zoé's clothes.

There was a scurry of rats as my lamp shed its light among the trunks and boxes, the barrels and kegs and ancient chests. Cobwebs hung from the rafters like the gray moss on the trees outside. Books and magazines that looked a century old were stacked in toppling piles. A dressmaker's dummy, a black, headless lady with full bust and tiny waist, stood guard over an empty cage that might once have housed a parrot. An old fishing net, weighted with bullets, hung on nails along the wall. A pair of oars leaned against a prostrate what-not. Everywhere broken furniture, gnawed by rats, bric-a-brac, old paintings and engravings, standing sideways or on their heads.

I set my lamp on a rickety table, wondering which of the

trunks to try first. I chose the smallest, since it looked as if it might have been Zoé's. It was not locked, but clamped tight like an oyster's shell. Suddenly it yielded, and a musty smell rushed out. There were only papers inside, yellow and crumbling, some with faded seals. The large cowhide trunk nearby was locked and impregnable, but a small black chest carved with dragons had no lock at all.

Dust, pale as sand, rose in a cloud as I lifted the lid. I wiped my hands on my handkerchief, almost overcome by a smell of camphor, and kneeling down, took out layers of blue paper, coming finally on ivory-colored cloth that I thought at first was damask, but found to be satin, heavy foldings that shone in the lamplight. It was not a dress, but cloth, that had been wrapped and laid away. Underneath was a lace reboso, white, too, such as the Spanish women wear. Beneath that lay a Chinese shawl, richly fringed, embroidered in red poppies.

These things didn't look like Zoé . . . But there were more. White kid slippers wrapped separately in the blue paper, long white kid gloves. A white prayer book, not wrapped at all . . . Was there a name in it? No, there was no name . . .

Suddenly I stopped, unable to move. I felt as if some one were watching me, standing close by. Indeed, it seemed to me there were shadows not made by my lamp, more blurred, more wavering . . . The blood had drained from my heart, but I must look. I must see what ghost had come without sound, and was waiting—for this, for me to find the strength to look around.

I lowered the lid of the chest and turned.

Ezra stood at the head of the stair.

In the flicker of his candle, his face, his mien appeared all Indian. He stood there, meeting my eyes, dark, impassive, silent.

I rose from my knees.

"I was looking for Miss Zoé's clothes."

Why did I feel I must explain to him?

His low monotone replied, "There is nothing of hers here."

Waiting. He stood motionless while the candle threw his gigantic shadow across the headless woman and up into the rafters.

I took my lamp and went past him down the stair.

Days later when again I tried the door to that stair I found it locked.

"Zoé," I said, "tell me about your dresses, the ones you lost."

Zoé, sitting on the floor among her shells, raised to me her sea-colored eyes.

"Those low, sneaking devils . . . They took my perfume, too—the *trefle incarnat*, my favorite. I don't smell it on them, they're too smart."

"What were they like—the clothes?"

She laid down the conch shell she had been holding to her ear.

"The dotted swiss was this color," pointing to the lining of the shell. "And the white mull was short-waisted." She stood up to show me. "With little puffed sleeves. I wore it with a leghorn hat and a sash of blue satin ribbon. Last year at school

I had a gray velvet, made princess style and silk-lined, and a silk petticoat underneath. The rustle was nice. All the girls rustled like that. And a yellow broadcloth cloak with a chinchilla muff and tippet. I pinned violets on the muff. The cloak came from Paris, and cost so much that Papa fussed. I had my picture taken in it . . . Where is my picture? *Where* is my—"

"What else, Zoé? What else did you have?"

"They've hidden my picture, too, the miserable—"

"Did you have any dress you specially liked?"

"Oh, yes, the handkerchief dress! You take chiffon handkerchiefs—big ones, big as bandannas, big as little shawls. You make the waist of one—you'll know how if you're smart. I'm not, but I could make the skirt. You take several of the handkerchiefs—a lot, I guess—and fasten each by one corner to the belt, all around the waist. Just leave them loose. It looks pretty when you dance."

She began to dance, skipping, twirling, floating out her skirt.

"My handkerchiefs are lilac and blue. First a lilac, then a blue, over a peach-colored petticoat. Madame Cluny in the village made it. She made the white mull, too. I'm going to wear the white mull when—"

She stopped as if she had said too much, and sat down again among her shells.

"Could you make a picture of the dresses?" I asked. "It might help me find them."

She accepted pencil and tablet and began to draw. I would say she had some gift for it. The outlines were distinct, the detail was clear. All at once she appeared to forget the dresses and began to doodle. Strange hybrid animals trailed from her pencil, birds with horns, a winged cow, fishes with whiskers, then a flock of faces that were neither beast nor human.

When she laid the pencil down I said, "Draw your bathing suit, Zoé—the one you lost."

She became interested again, remembering more and more, remembering even a dress she had wanted and not been allowed to buy. I decided to show these drawings to Judge Croome and ask if I might have them copied. He had instructed me to buy what I wished for Zoé, but since Ezra had surprised me in the attic I had been expecting a summons from Miss Johanna, and I wanted the judge's special support.

Only that morning, before her walk, I had taken Zoé to call on her father and on Miss Johanna. Miss Johanna had greeted me as always, yet I was certain that Ezra had made his report.

The judge looked the pictures over thoughtfully. He was not certain, he said, that my idea was a good one. However, there was a dressmaker in the village, a Mrs. Frisbie— Madame Cluny had died years before—and I might engage her to make a few of the garments, particularly the bathing suit, and see if they made Zoé any happier. He requested that I not tell Mrs. Frisbie for whom they were intended, and added that Ezra would take me in that afternoon, or, if I waited until tomorrow, I might go with Nannine when she did her marketing.

"Zoé will stay with me," he said.

Next morning Nannine and I left them sitting in the garden. Zoé knew nothing of my errand, had said no more about my looking for the dresses, seemed indeed to have forgotten

86

my promise to find them, as well as the pictures she had drawn. I took her measurements while she played abstractedly with the shells.

Nannine and I drove to the ferry, taking the station wagon. There was a touring car in the garage—the car I had arrived in—but it belonged to Richard Lowrie. The Croomes had no car besides the station wagon, and no need of any other.

I remember how warm the day was, and how sparkling the bay. I remember, too, that first glimpse of the village, its palm-shaded streets and tranquil houses, their gables or white pillars or widows' walks—those little railed platforms atop the roof, from which women had once watched for home-faring sails.

Purple and red bougainvillea climbed walls and fences. Oleanders grew tall and blossomed against the eaves. The men in their white linen suits walked more slowly than the men I had known, had more time for stopping, for chatting when they met. Pleasant and sweet-smelling, the village, a lady in full skirts, with flowers in her hair, dozing behind her fan.

Nannine left me among the shops while she did her marketing. Everything I saw I wanted for Zoé, but I must remember my errand. I found a dotted swiss among the curtain fabrics, a deeper pink than the conch shell's, and the dots probably too large. Chiffon I bought by the yard for the blue and lilac handkerchiefs, "big as little shawls." Pink taffeta I came on easily, and white mull, and blue satin ribbon.

"What's this?" inquired the dressmaker at sight of Zoé's drawings. "A fancy dress party?"

She was a thin, voluble, curious little person. When I answered yes, it was a fancy dress affair, she asked logically enough, "With all the guests the same size?"

On a side porch lay a brindle boxer dog, watching me narrowly through the open door.

"Don't mind Fo-Fum," Mrs. Frisbie said, looking over the drawings.

I asked if he were dangerous.

"Not any more," she answered. "He's been off the chain for years. But when I got him he was hardly human."

She held off a drawing and inspected it, her head on one side.

"Fo-Fum broke up a marriage," she said pensively. "The man was a sea captain, away for months at a time. Once, while he was gone, his wife got nervous and bought Fo-Fum to protect her, trained him to trust nobody and to bite anything that came near her. They say she didn't allow you even to say a kind word to Fo-Fum. Well, the captain came home, a perfect stranger, and Fo-Fum wouldn't let him get in bed with his wife. I understand the captain was very put out. Anyhow, they separated, and I was able to buy Fo-Fum cheap. He's had a very different sort of home with me. Anybody can pet him that wants to."

She began to laugh over Zoé's drawing of a bathing suit, hadn't realized that the beaches in her youth had been so comical. "Stockings and bathing shoes. Why not gloves and veils? Some of us did wear corsets in the water. Not girdles, steel-ribbed corsets. Hooked up in front, laced in back . . . I think it would be cute if we did this suit in bright red."

Sorry to dampen her enthusiasm, I showed her the navy blue alpaca and white braid Zoé had described.

"Very stodgy," said Mrs. Frisbie.

I departed from the orbit of Fo-Fum's vision with some relief. Nannine waited in the station wagon.

"I meant to caution you about that woman," she said. "If she begins to pry, just say, 'I don't know. Why do you ask?' That always stops them. 'Why do you ask?' "

We drove about the village, and into the Negro section. Nannine had brought a basket of Japanese persimmons for Belen. The old woman stood in the door of her house, a low brown cabin under a smother of Madeira vine. She saw the car and came down the walk, leaning on a cane. She came haltingly, black and wrinkled, a white cloth wrapped around her head. She peered curiously as Nannine introduced me.

"How Miss Zoé?" she inquired of Nannine. "Look like you ain't never gon' bring her to see me. Look like you promise and don't perform."

"Some day," said Nannine.

"I be gone some day," Belen answered. Again she looked at me. Tears were in her eyes, or perhaps just the rheum of age. "Maybe *you* bring her," she said.

Nannine produced the persimmons.

"Want me to carry them in, Belen?"

"No'am. Jest set 'em on the grass." She turned to me. "Give Miss Zoé my love. Please, ma'am."

I gave Zoé Belen's love. It was night. Zoé was in bed.

"Belen," she repeated, as if the name was new. Then, "Belen never tells," she said. "Belen is on my side. She's not afraid of Johanna. Where has Belen gone?"

89

"She's in her house in Muspa."

"When I go to Belen's house," said Zoé, "I play in the swing. Belen has a white cat, and her father sits outside in the sun and smokes his pipe. I play the harmonium, too, though I don't know how. I want to go to Belen's house."

"Perhaps it's different now."

"Why should it be different? Besides, I left my blue china cradle there. I was playing with it at the side of the house," Zoé sat up in bed, "and some dogs barked in the street, and the cat ran up the mulberry tree and wouldn't come down, and I forgot and left my cradle. I remember now. It's very little. Maybe Belen won't find it . . . Did you know that Belen is not afraid of Johanna, but Johanna is afraid of Belen? It was because of Belen they put in these bars. Belen was afraid I'd jump if Johanna dared me to again. Sometimes I did want to jump after Johanna dared me."

"When was that, Zoé?"

Her eyes clouded.

"I'm thinking. I'm remembering." Then suddenly, "Johanna came up here to the tower. I'll jump from most anything on a dare. I land light on my feet. Johanna dared me— there at the window. She dared me to jump. She was mad because I remembered something. I remembered it plain for a while, and she was mad. But she talked sweet to me, and said I wanted to jump, and dared me. I was all ready to jump when Belen came in. Johanna went out then, and I told Belen I had to jump because of the dare. And Belen told Papa, and Papa and Johanna said I had dreamed it, and Belen said it was true.

"Papa said there must be bars because I had jumping in my

mind. I hate the bars. I hate Johanna. When I go in to see her she says to me, 'You are crazy. You don't remember anything.' Over and over. 'You are crazy, crazy, crazy. You don't remember.' Her eyes hurt me. Like knives. If I had a knife . . ."

"Does your father know?"

"He says it's a dream. Maybe it is. Maybe it is . . . If I had a knife . . . I never can find a knife. A cord would do. Sometime when Johanna is asleep I'll tie a cord around her neck. A cord big as my little finger. I'll creep up soft, but it won't matter—she sleeps like the dead. I'll slip my cord around her neck and draw it tighter and tighter."

Zoé put her fists together, then slowly separated them, her full red lips pursed tightly, her eyes intent.

"That would be murder," I said.

"She might not die," lying down again, pushing the pillow firmly under her cheek. "She might just stop saying I'm crazy. No, she would die, and then the dream would stop . . . Do you think I'm crazy, Olive?"

"Certainly not."

"And I can remember. Please say to me that I do remember."

"You do remember, Zoé."

"There! That undoes the other. That undoes what Johanna says."

Zoé would never let me go with her to the clump of palms. We parted always at the cabaña. The cabaña had been built in the days of Yonder's gaiety, now it served merely as the spot where Zoé left me to keep her tryst with the sea. The length of the vigil varied, and I must be alert to the moment, if it came, when she walked into the water, must be close at hand.

We never conversed on our walks. They had one object, to reach the clump of palms. First would come her plea to walk on the bay side, then, when this was refused, the silent, eager journey to the palms.

But in the night we talked.

"Get in bed with me, Olive. Don't go yet."

And I would lie beside her, sometimes with my arms around her and her head on my shoulder, the length of her body pressed against me till she quieted.

"Are you married, Olive?"

"No, Zoé."

"Have you ever had a lover?"

She clung to me, her breath suspended. In the dark, against that continuous sound of washing sea, I heard the mesmeric ticking of the clock, and thought of the things Richard Lowrie had said about time.

"You have! *You have!*" whispered Zoé, holding me fast.

"No," I answered, "but I might have. There was a man I loved."

"Where is he now?"

"He married someone else."

"Oh . . . how can you live?"

"Somehow I do."

"You're smiling. I can tell."

"No, Zoé, I have you now. That's how I live."

92

"Tell me about him."

"There's nothing to tell. I just loved him."

"Did he love you?"

"I don't know."

She laughed, nestling close.

"How could you not know? He loved you. I tell you this. He loved you."

"Once I thought he did. But I don't know. I don't know anything except that it's hard to forget, even when there's nothing to remember."

"Poor Olive!" she sighed, and fell asleep.

X

There came a day when Nannine, spent from answering Miss Johanna's bell all night, asked me to do the marketing, since I was going into Muspa for the dresses Mrs. Frisbie had promised to have finished.

With a sense of freedom I climbed into the station wagon and drove aboard the ferry. The village was half asleep in the blazing afternoon, an even more endearing village, it seemed to me, on this second visit. I thought, driving under the palm trees, that I should like to live in Muspa, to know the people behind the white columns, under the gables and widows' walks.

Was I taking root, a severed thing like me, a thing that had no roots?

I stopped at the bank, Judge Croome having given me a check with instructions that I pay Mrs. Frisbie in cash. I stopped at the white-tiled market where the man in the big apron conferred with me over Nannine's list and stored Yonder's provisions in the station wagon. At last I drove to Mrs. Frisbie's cottage, mounted her porch, rang her bell.

"Oh, my dear, you're so early! I need another hour. Will you come in and wait?"

I said that I had another errand, and knew as I drove away that I had intended all along to call on Belen.

Belen's cabin, too, seemed asleep. Around the doorstone the bare ground had been swept clean. A few hens pecked in the shell-bordered flower beds. Half a coconut hull hung from the eaves, dribbling a green vine. Through the screen door I could see the scrubbed pine floor, the bed with its patchwork spread, the harmonium, the bureau and its mottled looking glass. The house seemed sentient, as if it breathed, and I knew someone was there.

I knocked again and heard the tap of Belen's cane. She came ponderously, the white cloth wrapped about her head, the rheumy eyes peering at me through the screen.

"I'm Miss Zoé's companion," I said.

She unhooked the screen door, drew forward a rocker, and when I had sat down, settled herself heavily in the straight chair beside the fireplace.

"Miss Zoé ain't sick, is she?"

I reassured her. Looking about the room I had discovered the object of my visit, a blue china cradle about eight inches long. It was on the mantelpiece with some withered pansies in it.

Old Belen sat studying me as she leaned forward, both hands on her cane. I doubt if she liked me very much. Perhaps she distrusted anyone who had taken her place on Yonder.

"Zoé told me," I said, "how she used to play the organ there. She remembers the white cat and your father."

95

"Was a time," said Belen, "when she didn't 'member nothin'."

"She's getting better," I answered. "She's going to get well."

Belen said nothing.

"You want her to get well, don't you?" I asked.

She blinked at me. "Does *you?*"

"I do, Belen."

"Miss Johanna say—the jedge say, too—she better like she is. She happy, they say."

"I know, but they're wrong. No one's better off in Zoé's state. And she's not happy because she knows she's not well. Do you know what it is she's trying to remember? It will help me if I understand. At least, I think it will help me. I want to do all I can for Zoé. That's what I'm here for."

The old woman sat staring out the door. I heard the clucking of the hens and a hum of bees through the window beside me. I heard the clock on the mantel and smelled the fragrance of some unfamiliar flower.

"I ain't know," said Belen.

"Weren't you there?" I asked.

She looked at me angrily. "No'am, I wasn't. Dan'l—he was the cook then—and Jessie and me, we all went to the carnival in Muspa. Jessie was the housemaid, and I took care Miss Johanna and Miss Zoé, kep' their clothes nice, and combed Miss Johanna's hair—it was so heavy she couldn't do it herself. Wasn't nobody there but Ezra. He was coachman then. Miss Zoé would a-told me when I come back, but she was dead— laid out on the bed like dead."

Silence, then the low voice went on.

96

"Twice a-fore I seed her like that, only not so bad. Once when she was little, and her mama died. Mizz Croome was a good lady. I worked for her fam'ly a-fore she married, come with her when she come to Yonder Key. Gentle and sweet, Mizz Croome, but her girls had wild blood in 'em. Diff'ent from her, and diff'ent from each other. Zoé was sweet inside like her mama, but wild as lightnin', ridin' that white horse like mad. She was her mama's pet, and Miss Johanna was her pa's. You could tell. And when Mizz Croome died Zoé skeered me to death, lyin' there like she dead, too. So weak when she come alive. Weak, and never sheddin' a tear."

The old woman wiped her eyes, then sat blinking at the door, leaning on her cane as if she would say no more.

"And the other time?" I said.

"Oh, yes'm—the other time was when Miss Johanna beat the horse. The white horse name Selim that belong to Miss Zoé. Miss Zoé was in Muspa that day, and Miss Johanna ride Selim and try to make him take a fence. He wouldn't do it, and she beat him till the blood come. Tied him to the fence and beat him with a rope. I seed him myself, blood all over his flanks. I seed the blood on her ridin' skirt when she got on him again and told him to jump the fence, and he done it and broke his leg.

"That's funny, too, 'cause I seed him take that fence with Miss Zoé lots of times—easy-like, 'cause he was a fine horse. He break his leg now with Miss Johanna, and she have him shot. Miss Zoé come home, and right away I tell her, and she run out—maybe she be in time; but no, she too late. She scream once, then all night she lay like she dead. She sick

97

when she come to this time, and when she get well the jedge send her off to school. She gone nearly a year.

"But this time—this last time, when Dan'l and Jessie and me come back from the carnival—I think Miss Zoé ain't gon' come to a-tall. When she do wake up she's crazy, scratchin' herself with her nails, and pullin' out her hair, and screamin' like it would tear out yo' insides. . . . She never tell us what happen. I ain't know."

Belen's voice had sunk to a mumble. She sat holding her cane, staring at the floor.

Did she really not know?

I waited, but she said no more.

"May I take the china cradle?" I asked. "Zoé remembers it. She wants it."

A light of cunning stole over Belen's face.

"You make 'em let Zoé come see me. I give her the cradle, myself."

"They would never bring her into Muspa," I answered. "You ought to know that."

"Then let 'em take me to her," said Belen. "I bring the cradle."

I promised to do my best, and rose. Belen unhooked the screen, and I went down the walk among the scratching hens.

The dresses had an unlooked-for effect on Zoé. That night when I came home I put them away, night being a bad time for excitement. Early next morning while she still slept I spread them on a chair beside her bed, the dotted swiss, the white mull, and a lace and nainsook petticoat that had been Mrs. Frisbie's own suggestion. Zoé was examining them when I came into her room, standing in her nightgown going minutely over every button, every ruffle. There was no excitement. She didn't ask where I had found them. They were merely there.

"Get your bath," I said. "We'll try them on, and see if they still fit."

"Of course they fit," she answered. "Why not?"

Why not, indeed? Her body melted into the dresses, gave itself to them in complete loveliness. The pink swiss had a pointed bodice and a full skirt that swept her insteps. She held it up a bit as she moved about the room, keeping in range of the long mirror. "I didn't know it was so long," she said.

The white mull she took in her arms, caressing its blue sash.

"He'll know me in this," she said. Then suddenly, "My hat! Did you find my hat?"

"Not yet. I'll try again."

"And my shoes. The high, buttoned ones. A white pair. A bronze pair. And evening slippers, silver kid. And black with red heels. But I need most the high buttoned ones."

"I'm afraid I can't find those, Zoé."

"Not even if I draw you a picture?"

"I'm afraid not. Besides, your feet won't show much. And anyhow you'll be wearing beach shoes."

"With this dress?" She looked at me astonished. "This is the day," she said.

"All right. Now we'll have breakfast."

Mrs. Frisbie had been especially curious the day before. Apparently she had seen and recognized Nannine on my first visit.

"How do you like Yonder?" she inquired, while Fo-Fum watched me from the porch as if interested in my reply.

"Very much," I said.

"Must be lonesome for a young woman like you. Is that funny one still alive?"

"Funny?"

"Crazy. The crazy one. I used to know the Croome girls. The younger one was pretty gay—wild in her ways, I mean. You know sex was more attractive in those days. It had mystery, was kept from girls like a beautiful secret, and if any of us peeped . . . Of course the clothes we wore look funny today, when everything's on display, when we hold nothing back in the way we dress, talk, and act. Sex is pretty shopworn."

"I see you're a philosopher."

"Well, but it's true. And what I miss most in these wide-open days is the risqué joke. The little witty, naughty joke. We used to laugh behind our fans, and get a real kick out of 'em. Nothing's risqué any more. We don't turn a hair at what we laughed at then. Why should we? A strip tease wouldn't excite a nudist colony."

I laughed, forgetting Fo-Fum, and asked if she knew that Bernard Shaw had predicted a return to clothes that concealed, a return in the interests of sex.

That would be all right, she said, if it could be done. She doubted if people ever returned to anything, especially to concealment after an era of exposure. I told her to read history, all the while helping her to fold the dresses, hurrying to get away before she mentioned Zoé again.

She asked quite suddenly,

"Was she really crazy—that younger Croome girl—or just so bad they had to cage her?"

"I don't know what you mean by 'bad.'"

"Why, what anybody means, I guess. But of course you weren't here then—weren't anywhere. Is it true they won't let the doctors see her?"

"I don't know that either," I said, and then, belatedly, "Why do you ask?"

Bad, I thought now, looking at that lovely face. "We were both wild for our generation," Helen Carrington had said. Wild, I told myself, as birds are wild. Innocent as the little risqué joke.

Zoé took off the dotted swiss, arrayed herself in the white mull with its high waist and small puffed sleeves. I tied the blue sash, letting the ends hang down the long flowing skirt. She pinned on the little bull's-eye watch.

"Please change your slippers, Zoé."

She refused. Not a practical beach attire, but she was happy.

We met no one as we went down the stairs and out of the house. Zoé had promised to be good if I would take her to the bay side. I had found that she kept any promise made the same hour. She stayed close to my side as we took the shell paths I had followed with Richard Lowrie. In the grove, the dark hollow where I had seen the egrets, she drew closer still, stopped and looked about her.

I felt it, too, a presence as pervading as the dark, as the

dank swamp smell. It seemed to press against us, to follow when we moved, to wait when we stood still. More palpable, more sinister than when I had been with Richard Lowrie.

I wondered if Zoé would turn back. Presently she raised her head and went on, that look of a sleepwalker on her face.

We came out into the sunlight. Ahead of us were the bay and the white coral rocks, the boathouse and straggling mangrove fence. Zoé caught my hand and ran, drawing me with her along a path that led into the cocal. Under the trees she slowed her pace, but, hurrying still, followed another path to the water's edge.

Here the reefs were shaped like stumps and covered with green slime. Sand flies buzzed over a dead sea gull and dumpings of refuse. An old rowboat had been beached and was falling to pieces.

Zoé looked around her. Things were not as she remembered them. She walked on, leaving me to follow, her skirts and ribbons fluttering in the salt breeze.

Ahead of us a sailboat rounded the island's curve, coming toward us. Zoé saw it at once, and stopped short. She raised a hand, waving. The boat came on, went past us.

"He didn't see me," she said, and turned back, keeping in a line with the boat, walking beside the rocks and mangroves. We arrived at the little mountain range of reefs near the boathouse. The sail went on ahead.

"Skee!" called Zoé. "Here I am! Skee!"

She waved a frantic hand. The man at the tiller waved back.

"That's a sponge boat," I told her. "It's going out to sea."

"Going to sea," she repeated. "He saw me, and he's going out to sea."

Her wild wet eyes followed the departing sail.

"Skee!" Her voice rang out over the bay. "Skee, don't go!"

The boat disappeared behind the trees.

"You're calling a sponge diver, Zoé. A strange man. What if he came?"

She twisted in my arms and was gone, was mounting the first reef, springing to a higher. Now she stood against the sky, her skirts, her hair, blowing, streaming back of her. I climbed after, calling to her as she had called the boat.

"Zoé! Zoé, come back! . . . Zoé, where are you?"

She had vanished. Now she reappeared, flying along the boathouse pier. At the pier's end she stood for a moment with stretched arms and pointed hands, then dropped into the bay and disappeared.

With the panic that takes us into fire or under traffic wheels, I all but plunged after her, I who had never dived in my life. I found myself scrambling down the reef, running back through the trees, finding—though I did not consciously remember where it stood—Richard Lowrie's house.

I heard the click of a typewriter as I rushed onto a screened veranda and through a doorway. A man sat at a table, a man with tanned bare torso and startled face. He rose and I saw that he had on shorts and espadrilles. I was not aware of these things then, but my brain kept somehow the picture of Richard Lowrie standing, looking at me. With what breath I had I gasped Zoé's name and said that she was drowning, or trying to, near the boathouse.

He shot past me, running along the path. I followed, coming out from the trees to see him an instant on the pier. Now they were both gone. The bay lay blue and quiet. Gulls wheeled, crying. Far off a boat called. It was as if nothing had happened. Yet Zoé was perhaps dead at the bottom of the bay, had risen her allotted three times, then gone down to die. Or it might be she had not risen at all, but had held onto the seaweed like someone I had once read about, determined to drown.

I went out on the pier to help if Zoé should be brought up. But when Richard appeared he was carrying her into the shallow water beyond the reefs.

XI

Zoé lay on the divan in Richard's house. Her eyes were open now, and she watched us as someone lying on the sea floor might watch the fauna of the region, passively, yet curiously, too, and not afraid. She did not know us, but our hands were ministering to her, and she had forgotten that she had tried to drown.

She had on a suit of Richard's pajamas. Her own clothes I had spread to dry on the bushes outside. Rory, Richard's Irish setter, lay on the floor beside her.

Richard's house was a place of windows and screened veranda, of patio and jalousied breezeway, of low, overhanging roof. The tiled floors were strewn with mats, and the living room looked as if nothing but a man and a dog had ever been inside it. Books and maps were scattered about, and on a table was an enormous globe. There were cushioned rattan chairs, a radio and a typewriter.

Richard was in fresh shorts and polo shirt, his dark hair wetly brushed. He had been absent from the room and returned now with hot popovers and a pot of coffee, fresh butter and seagrape jelly. Zoé's eyes came alive as he set a table beside the divan. "I'll pour the coffee," she said, and sat up.

I wondered that they could either of them eat. Inside me was a tremor that I believed would never stop. If Richard had not been there, Zoé would have drowned, and I would have been to blame. I felt that I could never take her out again, certainly not to the bay side. She was much craftier, much stronger than I had realized.

She sipped her coffee, a pale, small Pierrot in the big pajamas. Her eyes grew dreamy, and she gazed at Richard. She knew us now.

"The shirt was burning. Tell Olive."

Richard handed me the cream, sat down again.

"The shirt," repeated Zoé. "Tell Olive."

"That's her favorite story," Richard said.

"He was twelve," said Zoé, "and the stern-kicker was named *The Pioneer*."

"You are mistaken," said Richard. "I was fifteen."

"I know. But then there was less excuse."

"No excuse at all."

. "Except the crabs," said Zoé.

"Right. I was stone-crabbing. I broke my propeller and was drifting out to sea."

"Out to sea," repeated Zoé. She put down her cup and rose, her eyes on the open door. I laid a hand on her arm. She stared at me.

"Stay and hear Richard's story," I begged, and he added, "I can't tell it without you."

That, she felt, was true, and sat down again.

"You broke your propeller," I reminded Richard. "What happened then?"

"A junk," said Zoé, pouring more coffee all around.

"A junk," echoed Richard. "In the distance. I raised my shirt on an oar, and set it afire."

Zoé did not help him, though he paused. She leaned back on the divan and ate her popover.

"The junk bore down on me," related Richard, "and I was rescued. Had to abandon *The Pioneer* which was half full of water. Gave my crabs, a bushel basketful to the man in the junk, an old navigator, making his last trip, writing a book about sharks. He started me off on my own tack. My father expected me to be a doctor. I expected it, too. So I had to go out on the open sea and meet a man who was writing a book about sharks."

"Destiny, you mean."

Yes, he had meant that. But he would have made a good doctor.

After the popovers Zoé lay back on the divan and fell asleep. The bull's-eye watch slipped from her hand, falling on the rug. I picked it up, surmising that it was probably none the worse for its dunking, since it had long ago stopped running. How exquisite it was. How like Zoé herself, with all its little wheels gone wrong.

I laid it on the mantel, out of harm's way, and went out among the shrubbery to gather up her clothes. Richard joined me, took me around his place, showed me the cement-lined pool with the plank floating on it so that birds and raccoons might drink, showed me his solar heater with its coil exposed to the sun, giving him hot water at all times.

He behaved as if no near-tragedy had occurred, did not reproach me for bringing Zoé to the bay side. I was calmer because of his attitude. Certainly reproaches would have been superfluous. It would never happen again.

I told him about Zoé's new dresses and my visit to Belen, of how Belen wanted to come and see Zoé. I said that I had meant to speak of it to Judge Croome, but doubted now that I would. If he had wanted Belen to visit Zoé, he would have arranged it long ago.

"That doesn't follow," Richard said. "He may not have thought of it. How could it hurt Zoé?"

"It might disturb her memories."

He said after a moment, "Zoé's getting better."

"Better when she tried to drown herself?"

"She's always done that," he answered. "Today she all but succeeded. She may not do it again."

Still, I felt that I would not urge a visit from Belen. I would bring the rest of the dresses from Muspa, but I would do nothing more on my own where Zoé was involved.

She was awake when we came in, playing on the floor with Rory. I wandered among Richard's bookshelves, glancing at atlases and fathograms, at treatises on forestry and tropical farming, on ecological animal geography and the global thermostat. Suddenly in a corner I came on titles of his own, and asked the loan of his last one, *The Dry Tortugas*. I got Zoé into her dress for the walk home. Richard went with us to the door of the tower room.

But in the night I dealt with Zoé alone, as perhaps I deserved to do. I lay awake a long time, quieting my nerves with Richard's book, visiting that island set in amethyst water, where the bones of old wrecks lay on the white mud, and great birds with wings like sails flew screaming over the tide riffs.

Zoé slept soundly, now that she slept. There was not even a sound of breathing from her room, or the rambling murmurs that sometimes accompanied her sleep. There was nothing in all the world but that wash of the sea beyond my windows, and the still, full moon.

Suddenly the night was split with a scream so terrible that I lay frozen. It was the cry of an agonized beast, not Zoé.

When I reached her side she was sitting up in bed, her fingers clutched in her hair. The moon was like day in the room.

"Go away!" she screamed at sight of me.

I sat beside her. "It was a dream, Zoé."

She pressed her head against my arm. "I saw," she whispered. "I went through the door. I saw, but I lost it."

"Well, let it go. You don't want it. Go back to sleep."

She lay down, but it was not until dawn that she slept again.

No, I would do no more to help Zoé get well.

A letter from Helen Carrington.

How are things with you? I hear very seldom from Uncle Heber or Johanna. I realize that I haven't answered your last letter, but don't, dear, wait for me. Our family is poor in letter writers.

I hope you still like Yonder, and that the change has

109

been good for you. Give my love to Zoé. I believe she'll understand.

Pony is still in Paris, getting her fill of gaiety. In my dreams at night I see her whirling in full tulle skirts like a ballet dancer, eyes bright, cheeks flushed—perhaps because that was the way I saw her last, at her party. Her father disapproves of her divorce from Thad, though he was never reconciled to her marriage. I didn't tell you at the time—you were in so much trouble—but my aunt whom Pony is named for, Uncle Heber's sister, Josephine, died last fall and left Pony all her money. She was a quiet, conservative soul. Little she knew what Pony would do.

Dane has left the bank and gone into Mr. Roy's textile business. Leonie is expecting a baby. She's very good for Dane. He's always been humored, not by his father, of course, but by everyone else, including himself. Imagine Leonie humoring anybody! Dane seems to be a model husband, and now with the baby coming . . .

I laid the letter down.

Dane a father. Dane with a child, blond and shining like himself, or dark like Leonie . . . Dane in a role that I could not imagine him in.

The little boy on the beach—a familiar figure now, running, wading, digging in the sand—appeared again that evening, trudged home through the afterglow.

He never came again.

XII

That week I went into Muspa with Nannine and got the rest of Zoé's dresses. Zoé, to my surprise, gave me her watch, asking me to have it regulated. She had always insisted that it kept perfect time. Now she was not so sure.

I remember the jeweler's delight in Zoé's treasure, in the oddly cut diamonds that composed the bow-knot pin. It was a foreign watch, he said, delicate—an heirloom, no doubt—and had been much abused. The repairs would take time. I made a special trip later to retrieve the watch, Zoé missed it so, and when it was in her hands again her gratitude was overwhelming.

"If I die first, Olive," she said, "I'm going to will you this watch. No one else shall have it. Only you."

I had found also some pink clover perfume—her favorite—at the dime store and the room was redolent with it.

"Now I feel right," she said. "Now I feel like myself."

The things from Mrs. Frisbie included three dresses—a yellow organdie, the handkerchief dress, an apple-green muslin—and the bathing suit. In the bathing suit she skipped along the sand, a comic figure, except for her delight and grace.

We went into the water together, I in the suit she had refused as indecent, and which she noticed on me not at all. She swam, she floated, she rode a great plastic dolphin that Richard Lowrie had brought from Muspa. Richard joined us in the water, and that day Zoé did not sit and watch beneath her palm trees, but walked home contentedly between us.

Richard had come to invite us to his house for the afternoon. A party, he said.

Zoé chose to wear the yellow organdie, a thing of flounces with a square-necked bodice. Her long gold hair she combed into a "psyche" on top of her head. In my short frock, with my smooth dark bob, we must have been a contrasting pair as we took the beach road, a route that Richard had shown me that day, saving me the path through the grove. Pink flamingoes argued with us the right of way, and we heard the chattering of the green parakeets and saw them clinging in flocks to Richard's eaves.

He came with Rory to meet us, escorted us to the door. In the living room I saw at first no one at all, then my eyes made out a shape in one of the deep chairs, bowed, amorphous, her head wrapped in a white cloth.

"Belen!" cried Zoé, and ran toward her, was lost in her arms.

Richard drew me outside, leaving them alone. I saw Hiram's younger son, Floyd, as we went past the kitchen.

"He'll get dinner for them," Richard explained. "You and I are taking the launch for the mainland."

The bay was a fine blue that waning afternoon, with almost

no breeze. We circled the island, then headed for a point on the mainland, barren except for a pier and a low, weathered tavern called the Barnacle.

Over the conch chowder Richard talked about the yawl, in drydock now, waiting till he should set out for Damballa Oueddo.

"Where's that?"

"Off the coast of Africa. I've got to find it."

"Is it lost?"

That smile in his eyes. "It's not on the map—not yet."

"It sounds like the end of the world. I suppose it's a paradise."

"I doubt it. Volcano and jungle and deep black canyons. Some sailors were shipwrecked on its coast. That's how we know it's there."

"Any natives?"

"Savages. They dye their bodies yellow and paint white rings around their eyes. The island is named for their voodoo god, and they're served by a race of pygmy slaves. The women speak one language and the men another."

"They seem to have thought of everything. Would you take a crew of one?"

"I might. There's an extra bunk. Can you handle a tiller?"

"Yes, and reef a sail. And bail water. And cook."

Well, he said, since I was coming along he'd make it Eleuthera, instead.

"That's the Bahamas, a short trip, one I've had in mind a long time."

"Eleuthera." I liked the sound.

"It means 'do as you please.' Some disappointed people

113

settled it three centuries ago. Moved from England to Bermuda, and from Bermuda there. Idealists, scholars, adventurers. A colony founded on discontent. I'd saved Eleuthera for my later years, but if you're coming, too—"

"Did they find what they wanted?"

"Some did. The rest moved on—to Florida. Here in the keys they seem to have stayed. You run across old Conchs with a courtesy and a religious zeal, handed down from Eleutherian forebears. I've noticed something of the kind in Hiram, in Floyd, too. They come from Key West, but if they're descended from the Eleutherians, they don't know it. . . . When do we start?"

We both smiled. "I mustn't divert you from your voodoo island. Somebody else might find it, and put the natives to weaving baskets. How long will you be gone?"

He didn't know, looking at me pensively. Couldn't make plans till his present book was out of the way.

We talked on through the bollos and broiled crawfish, through the salad and lime pie. It grew dim in our booth beside the open window, and the waiter lit the candles in their pewter holders, cleared the red-checked cloth, brought the coffee. Outside, the sun dyed to orange the sails about the pier. There was the rhythmic rush and hush of the sea, its harsh salt smell, that were beginning to be a part of me. I should miss them if ever I went away . . . If ever I went —where?

"What is it, Olive?"

Richard was leaning both arms on the table, looking at me, the line deep between his brows, though he was not frown-

114

ing. "What is it you're thinking about when you get that look on your face?"

"Did I get a look?"

"Yes, and I've seen it before, a look as if you were lost. What are you thinking at these times?"

"Not always the same thing, I imagine. Right then I was wondering where I'd go if I ever left Yonder."

"Home," he suggested.

So no one had told him. Oddly enough, I had supposed he knew. I told him now. It was not hard, and grew easier with the telling, as if something that had bound me tight began to loosen. The twilight came as we sat there. The orange sails faded to mauve and then became shadow until small jewel lights pricked their outline on the dark. Chinese lanterns kindled along the pier, music began there, and dancing. Voices called and answered. A motor boat muttered and was still . . . All so far away, another world that we heard and saw from our dark star.

How quietly he listened to me, saying at last that it was better—though apparently no such alternative had threatened in my case—to see one's parents go like that than by prolonged suffering. "I think you wouldn't trade your cup for mine," he said, "though mine is rather average."

Perhaps not, I thought. Yet he hadn't cracked as I had cracked. Perhaps he had more stamina, more equilibrium, or else we need some preparation for our cup.

"Don't think I don't understand," he said. "I do. Lost look and all."

"It's not that I think about it a lot," I answered. "I don't—

not since I came here and had Zoé to think about. What's back of Zoé, what she went through, must have been worse. Miss Johanna said an odd thing in her talk with me," I broke off, wondering what explanation he might offer. "She told me not to pray for Zoé."

"And have you?"

"Never. When I've wanted to I've always heard that voice commanding me not to."

"Sounds like hypnotism."

"It is, I imagine. I'm sure she exercises some definite hypnotic power. Dane Carrington, her cousin, spoke of it. He visited Yonder as a child, and told me that he remembered her eyes, that he had been afraid of them."

"Were *you* afraid?"

"Yes, I think when I talked with her I was afraid—of losing my own will, or something of the sort. I know Zoé's afraid."

"I knew a man once," Richard said, "a British soldier, bound for service in India. They were training him to combat just that—hypnotism, the deceptions, that is, of the necromancers. They told him that instead of armoring himself in will power, he should relax and keep some fact or truth in mind. 'Take one from the Bible,' they said. 'Take "Blessed are the peacemakers." ' The guy said he didn't believe in the Bible, so they told him to take another great fact. 'Take two and two is four. And hold to it.'

"He told me that during his exam a plate of fruit appeared suddenly before him. Two and two is four, he thought, and the plate fell to the floor, and shattered, scattering the fruit. Then the pieces of the plate came together again, the fruit rolled back into it, and rose up in front of him, more luscious than ever. But my friend who said he had never felt hungrier in his life, kept saying his two-times-two till it disappeared.

"He passed his test, and got on all right with the wizards in India . . . If you want to pray for Zoé, don't let Miss Johanna stop you."

"Well, she has. If Zoé gets well it will be without any prayers of mine, without anybody's prayers, I guess. When I first came to Yonder I was prayerless. Then not long ago I began to pray that I'd do the right thing by Zoé. That was all. And then I nearly let her drown."

"Zoé was taken care of," he said.

"Thanks to you."

"Who knows? I had a message that morning calling me down the coast, had expected to go, decided not to. Mightn't that have been your prayer?"

Down the coast. He had been down the coast that first night, the night he met my train. Often he was away—perhaps down the coast. Was there some woman whom he went to see? . . . Silently I visualized her, poised and with blue eyes, since his were dark; fair hair smoothly coifed, and cool hands, a dress that clung and flowed in lovely lines. I could see her smile, welcoming him into her beautiful home . . . Why was he not married? How had he escaped? Perhaps she had a husband . . .

"Odd." His voice called me back. "I'm not intuitive, at least, I think I'm not. When people talk about auras—a woman's aura changing after certain experiences, I'm rather in the dark. Maybe I haven't thought about it much, or believed enough in auras. Still, I get from you a feeling of— Oh, a warning, something that says, 'Walk softly. Take care.

Something's buried here, something that was alive.' I put it badly, but it's what I mean."

"Something's buried," I said after a moment, looking out into the dark. I managed a smile. "That's it . . . X marks the spot. I buried it in myself."

"Does the ghost walk? Inside you, I mean."

"Yes, of course. It has nowhere else to walk. I never thought of that before."

I told him about Dane. Not all, most of it.

To the good listener, as had once been pointed out to me, people tell more than they intend. He heard me thoughtfully, the rough lock dropping over his forehead, the candle etching his face in planes of light and shadow, a face by Rembrandt. He said after a silence,

"The experience has been all inside yourself. That's why the mark on you has been so definite, as definite as a marriage, more definite, perhaps. If a man should knock on your door —a man who had ignored all outside warnings—the ghost would send him away."

"Oh, no." The picture was amusing. I had to smile.

"Yes. And if he took you on such a journey as we were dreaming about a minute ago, the ghost would come along, a third passenger . . . Is he happy in his marriage, this Dane Carrington?"

"I think so. There's a child coming. I haven't seen him since I heard that. I mean I often used to see him on the beach, speaking of ghosts. Only he was a little boy, because I saw him as he was when he was here. He told me about it, and I saw him as he was then, only not any more."

"I suppose the Freudians would make something of that,"

Richard remarked, "your seeing him as a child. Seeing him as a little boy."

I wanted him to go on, to explain, but he stopped and was silent.

And suddenly I heard the music again, and saw the dancers out on the pier.

It was night when we returned to Yonder. Zoé, on the mat beside Belen's chair, was rocking the blue cradle, singing to it. Belen got to her feet and went with Floyd down the path to the launch. Richard took us home by the beach road.

That night in a dream I was on the high seas with Richard. A rough ocean and a bank of cloud that darkened as we advanced. Where we were bound seemed not to matter, but there was a storm coming, and the boat was heeling to starboard. Frantically I was trying to cook, standing at an angle of forty-five degrees. Great waves came over the boat, and Richard at the tiller called to me, "Bail! Bail!"

I knew where to find a pail and shovel and, going to fetch them from beside the extra bunk, I found a child sitting in the bunk, a little fair-haired boy in yellow swimming trunks. He laughed when I tried to cover him, to hide him from Richard. But Richard saw, and cried out, "Stowaway!"

Suddenly we were all three in the water, and Richard was swimming toward me to save me, and I was trying to save the child who kept disappearing under the waves. The waves were black. They were overwhelming. They were too terrible, and I woke, thankful for the moonlight, for the tranquil murmur of the seas against Yonder.

XIII

Winter had dissolved into spring, almost imperceptibly. The visiting birds, mute while with us, had departed for their homes. The mockingbird, branded as a plagiarist, sang on, the sweetest singing ever done by bird. How could he mock the visitors whom he had never heard? Indeed, I wondered if it was not they who learned of him, listening silently in the covert of the leaves, airing his trills and cadenzas when they got back home.

Richard taught me the birds. Before they left we roved among the keys, wearing snake boots and jeans, carrying our spy-glasses. In moss-hung caverns of shadow we came on a rookery of ibises, or a colony of roseate spoonbills, or of coots too fat to fly. Marsh hawks, grebes and kingfishers haunted the winding waterways and tiny islands that fringed the nether shore of Yonder, water turkeys and meadow larks. Sometimes we met an alligator, or a raccoon waddling down to fish.

He taught me the trees that I had never felt at home with —the soursop and the gumbo limbo, the sandbox tree with its onion-shaped fruit that explodes violently when ripe; the lebbek whose powder-puff blossom seduces with its perfume, then hardens into a long bean that rattles in the wind and is known as the woman's tongue.

There were flowers, lush and fantastic, or pale, starry and secret, glimmering at the edge of pools. There were a thousand fragrances haunting the shadow, and there were carnival-colored moths and butterflies with many-syllabled names. There was the deadly beauty of the coral snake and the jeweled black tarantula, and the machineel tree whose golden apple and whose very dew is poison.

In Richard Lowrie's kitchen Floyd taught me to skin a jewfish and to pickle limes in sea water. Zoé, too, learned these things, only to forget them by nightfall, while Richard, shut in his study, worked on his book, insisting that he liked to have us there, joining us when the day's stint was over.

One morning he took us fishing on Lonely Key. We invited Nannine, whose day off it was, but remembering the rattler, no doubt, she chose to visit Muspa instead.

It was a blowing day, salty and cool, with only a few puffs of cloud in the sky. Here and there was a fishing boat or a loitering white sail. The world seemed bright as a new coin, and nothing in the wind but good.

Floyd caught us a pail of sardines and pilchers for bait while Richard checked the gas and went over the *Blade*. Floyd brought, too, a frying pan and a coffee pot, a basket of coconut fiber stored with fresh bread and butter, with pickles and condiments, and at Zoé's request, a chocolate cake. He had packed the salad in one of the loaves of bread, had sliced off the top to make a lid, and hollowed out some of the crumb, and there our lettuce and tomatoes remained as fresh as when they were put in.

Between Beacon Key and Lonely we dropped anchor and cast our handlines. I don't know why Zoé caught more than anybody else, only that it made her gleeful. Snappers and runners, porgies and yellowtails and little orange-mouthed grunts. Some we would fry for lunch, and some we would take back home, and the grunts we would feed to Cato, the pelican, who lived on Lonely and who always came out to greet the fishers.

He came today, perching on our moored boat, eating greedily, then, swollen and sleepy, watched us land.

Lonely was mostly jungle, but there was a leaning old jetty and a fine beach. Richard cleaned three of the snappers, and we built a fire, eating our lunch under the palm trees. We brought the dozing Cato to join us, and he sat at the head of the table, stuffed to the ears, blinking at our laughter. Richard, who had brought his camera, snapped Cato's picture, snapped mine too, sitting beside him. After lunch, in much the same state as Cato, we lay on the sand for naps, while gulls flew creaking in the blue, blazing quiet, and the tide came in.

Only Richard slept, his lean brown length stretched in the palm shade. Zoé flitted away, gathering shells, then while I watched her, slipped into the jungle. Once before lunch she had done this, and I had followed. In that tangle of thorn-bush and screwpine she had milled about as if lost, and I finally drew her out again. Now as I joined her, we stumbled on a path, and she suddenly ran along it, leading the way, jumping over rocks and vines, pushing branches aside.

There was no stopping her now, though we were not dressed for jungle travel, but in shorts and halters. The briars and nettles scratched our legs, and, unless I was alert, the boughs, as Zoé released them, flew back into my face. I thought of Nannine's rattler, and while I was certain that Richard had seen us leave, I was equally sure that we had gone too far for him to hear us if we screamed. Still, I almost wished for a snake, doubting at the same time that it would stop Zoé in her headlong flight.

She did stop, however, and I saw that we had arrived at a house, a small place built of mildewed coral rock, almost hidden by the trees. Its walls were spotted with fungi, its blinds were closed. Asleep, dead, here in the heart of the jungle.

Zoé was trying the door, turning, turning the knob.

"It's locked," she said.

"Come on then," I begged. "Come, Zoé."

She neither heard nor saw me, but jumped off the porch and went around to the side. I followed more slowly through the thorns and brambles. I had seen that her arms and legs were bleeding, though she did not know.

She had found an unlocked back door that gave as she pushed. No use to plead with her now, or command. She simply did not hear. I stood with her in a dank and musty kitchen. She opened a cupboard drawer and took out a candle. "Matches, matches . . ." She found those, too, most of them too damp to strike. At last one flared, and she lit the candle, went into the other room, a room with bunks. Fishing tackle was piled in a corner. The grate was full of dead ashes, and the smell of mold and damp almost overpowering.

"Come, Zoé. You've seen inside now. Let's go."

She sat down on one of the bunks, holding the candle, her eyes large and bright.

"Zoé, Richard will be worried."

I took the candle away from her and blew it out. Then, just when I thought she was coming with me, she lay down on the bunk and turned her back to me.

"Zoé, this place is filthy—can't you see? Those old blankets—"

She put her arms around the pillow, buried her face in it.

"All right," I said. "I'm going to leave you. I'm going back to the boat."

It was useless. She lay perfectly still as I went toward the door, which after all I could not open—an old-fashioned lock, and no key in it. I turned back and waited in the kitchen.

After a time she came. We went slowly down the path and out onto the beach where Richard, having packed our gear, was watching for us with some impatience. A squall was headed our way, he said, and hurried us aboard the *Blade*. We raced a chill wind under darkening skies, landed on Yonder just in time, flying to Richard's house where Rory greeted us with what appeared to be relief, and Floyd had a log fire and hot drinks waiting.

Now the rain broke, lashing the roof, pouring into the gutters along the eaves. The trees wrestled with one another, and the sea stood up and roared. I thought of the night I came, and wondered if they were worried about Zoé at the house. Probably not, since Richard was with us.

The radio was full of static, though music from Cuba filtered through now and then. The rain became bells on the roof, then muted to a drone. Richard threw driftwood into the fireplace and the flames ran over it, blue and orange and green. Zoé sat close to the hearth on a three-legged stool, her hair tinged with the colors of the fire. There was something eerie, something magic in the picture. I think Richard felt it, too, for he brought a volume of Yeats and asked me to read aloud. I knew he was thinking of *The Land of Heart's Desire* where nobody gets old and crafty and wise, so I read to him about the elf girl, swaying and singing with the reeds, always a child. He listened, lounging back in his chair, while the rain drummed, and Zoé on her stool with Rory at her feet, clasped her hands about her knees and watched the fire.

Richard asked for the one beginning, "When you are old and gray . . ."

When you are old and grey and full of sleep,
And nodding by the fire, take down this book
And turn the leaves, and dream of the soft look
Your eyes had once, and of their shadows deep . . .

How many loved your moments of glad grace,
And loved your beauty with love false and true,
But one man loved the pilgrim soul in you
And all the sorrows of your changing face . . .

"What color are your eyes, Olive?"
Richard speaking softly like somebody at a concert.
I laughed, losing the mood of the poem.
"They're smoky hazel," said Richard. "Go on, I didn't mean to interrupt."

Zoé began to cry. She looked from Richard to me, her tears twinkling blue and green. She covered her face, and Richard signaled me to go on, to pay no attention.

The sun was setting in a clear sky as we walked home.

XIV

Miss Johanna never undertook to train me for handling Zoé, as she had promised to do the night I came, though I had certainly expected to be summoned by her for something more radical than instruction—for dismissal, even, after my encounter with Ezra in the attic.

On Sundays I went to church with Nannine, and afterward there was dinner with Miss Johanna and her father. Often Richard joined us at the long table with its ecclesiastical gold candlesticks, and the meal was considerably livelier when he did. The judge was undeniably fond of Richard, and emerged somewhat from his lethargy on these occasions. Miss Johanna sat grimly in her place, speaking generally of the limes, which, with the breadfruit and the Madeira grape, were the chief crop of Yonder.

Always, going downstairs, I felt Miss Johanna's unseen presence, and now and then I met her in the halls, an erect figure propelling her wheel chair from one vast room to another, on the trail of some bit of dust or disorder. We would pass each other and as she gave her stiff nod in answer to my greeting, she kept her black eyes focused straight ahead. In time I came not to speak as we met in this fashion, pretending in the twilight of the hall not to see her. I gathered somehow that she liked this better.

She did not invite me in when I went with Zoé to her door, following our weekly visit with Judge Croome. The judge, on the other hand, was hospitable, having developed a desire for conversation, seeming disappointed whenever I preferred to wait for Zoé in the garden. It was only when I felt equal to his questions that I remained with her in his office. There, I sat in the love seat under the portrait of his wife, a grave and sweet-faced lady, blonde as Zoé, dressed in mauve satin, with yellow roses in her lap.

The judge was curious about my father and the people of his parish; more curious about the Carringtons. What was Dane like? Pony? ("She was named for my sister, Josephine. And Josephine left her everything.") Fritz? ("I have never seen Fritz. I should like to see Fritz.")

He was avid of anecdote. I racked my brain for remembered incidents, small happenings in the lives of the Carrington children, our adventures on the lake, at the farm. Nothing was too slight to interest him, and I came to know when he was beguiled, for at these times the look of brooding would lift from his face, and his torpid eyes grow bright.

In return he confided in me, told me what to him was a matter of secrecy and excitement. They were experimenting on Yonder with the carnauba, the South American palm which yields the wax essential to airplanes, a thin coating on the wings making them impervious to water.

"In Brazil," he said, "this palm is so prized that the law forbids sending out the seed. Richard brought ours from British Guiana. Our plants have put forth a second character leaf in ten months, a real achievement."

He spoke softly so that even Zoé might not overhear.

His sight was too poor for reading, for writing, so that I wondered what he did at his desk with its spread of papers. The radio brought him little of interest besides the news. Our visits were what he looked forward to, though Zoé would willingly have dispensed with them. Only when the dresses were new did she seem eager to call on her father. On Johanna, too. She wanted Johanna to see the dresses, to know that they had been found. In the judge's office she would sit with her full skirts spread around her, a glowing object in that somber room. Dress after dress for his admiration. Even the bathing suit. In the bathing suit she perched on his desk, an imp, a gargoyle. She skipped in a ring around the smiling old man.

"Dance! Dance!" she cried, and grasped his hands, and capered circling, while he took small toddling steps, still smiling, revolving where he stood.

What took place when Zoé called on Miss Johanna I could only guess. Once, uneasy, I returned ahead of schedule, and as I waited outside the door I heard Zoé moaning, a sound like the whine of an animal with its foot in a trap. Miss Johanna was talking, and while I could not distinguish her words, the tone was even and not unpleasant, a sort of chant, with this agonized whine as its accompaniment. Suddenly there was a scream, a yell—not Zoé's—and I opened the door.

Miss Johanna sat crouched in her wheel chair, her hands

over her face. Zoé, standing close to her, turned and looked at me.

"Take her out!" screamed Miss Johanna, removing her hands. Her face was bleeding.

I brought water and a fresh towel. The triple red stripes might have been made by a tiger.

"Take her out," Miss Johanna cried again, holding the towel against her face. "Ring for Nannine."

The bell buttons were beside her bed. I touched the one marked Nurse, and went out with Zoé.

We had called first on the judge, but he was in conference with Hiram. Hiram was gone now, and the judge admitted us. Zoé, always disorganized after her sessions with Miss Johanna, was today incoherent. The judge questioned me, and I could tell him only what I had heard and seen, not omitting Miss Johanna's scratched face. He looked sadly at Zoé, blaming her, and Zoé, who had found a moth at the window, played with it and seemed not to care.

I said that I knew she had acted in reprisal or self-defense. The old man shook his head. "Reprisal for what? Defense against a woman in a wheel chair?"

I thought, Why don't I speak out? What's stopping me?

"Does Miss Johanna want Zoé to get well?" I asked. "Do you?"

He sank down into the easy chair, became a part of it, bowed his great condor head.

"You don't know what you say, Miss York. We do all we can for Zoé."

"Then why does Miss Johanna constantly remind her—

Why does she say to her, 'You don't remember. You are crazy'?"

"Did you hear her say these things?"

"No, I am not permitted to go in with Zoé when she visits her sister, and these visits must always come after Zoé has been with you, not before, as it was today. There must be a reason for that."

"I'm not crazy," said Zoé, turning from the moth. "Say that I'm not."

"She dreams these things," said the judge. "A persecution complex. The commonest symptom."

"I think they're true," I said. "Belen says they're true."

"Ah . . . Belen," shaking his bowed head.

I felt suddenly furious with him, refusing to see, to act.

"In any case," I said, "if Zoé continues to see her sister, I'm leaving."

I hadn't expected to say that. I stood for a moment watching his head sink lower, then I took Zoé by the hand and went out.

There was something that I had told no one, worrying over it alone. One day in Zoé's room the string of my amber beads had broken, and gathering them up, searching for them, I found under the edge of the rug a short knife with a rusty blade. I recognized it as one that she had picked up on the beach, some sailor's knife washed up by the tide. Zoé had studied it curiously, had watched with regret when I threw it back into the waves.

Where and when had she found it again? Perhaps it had

been lying at low tide under her clump of palms, conniving with her in whatever she had in mind. I took the knife out and buried it in the black leaf-mold of the grove, and the fact that she did not ask for it or seem to miss it quieted my fears.

Yet I knew that inside her lurked the intent to kill. She had spoken to me once about a rope, had illustrated the act of throttling, putting her fists together, drawing them rigidly apart. With every visit to Miss Johanna, she was being driven further into her darkness, and in that darkness she was plotting a way to destroy her tormentor.

I was watching her carefully now, hurrying out with the dishes after our meals, lest she steal a plate and break it into a weapon. The glass in the bathroom I replaced with a plastic cup, and remembering Jael in the Bible, I removed the nail on which a solitary picture hung, hiding the picture, leaving a hole in the plastered wall for Nannine to inquire about, though she hadn't yet.

That Zoé's mania had become homicidal was a problem that I had buried as deep as I buried the knife, though it would have been a relief to share it with Richard. Richard seldom hung fire about things. It was his way to move. In the case of Belen he had gone and got her. In this matter, too, he would undoubtedly move, and probably in a direction I didn't want, might even say, "You are not safe yourself." He would talk with Judge Croome, no doubt, and they would imprison Zoé, perhaps take away her walks, get her a guardian who, they felt, would be less gentle with this mania, sending me away—all this being precisely what Johanna Croome had in mind.

All the situation needed, I told myself, was for Zoé to discontinue her visits to her sister. But my ultimatum to Judge Croome was as much of a surprise to me as it had been to him. Perhaps, indeed, he would take me at my word and let me go.

Shall I ever forget that night? We ate our supper in a silence unmarred even by the phonograph which usually poured out ancient waltzes or ragtime during our meals. Zoé got into bed early, leaving me free to do the same. I was restless, however, and kept seeing Miss Johanna's scratched face and hearing her scream. At last, however, lulled by that eternal wash of the sea, I fell asleep.

I woke with a feeling of apprehension, looked at the illuminated dial beside my bed. Two o'clock. No sound from Zoé's room. Even so, I went to see if all was well.

She was not in her bed, nor in the bathroom. Her door into the hall stood open. That meant she had taken the key from beneath my pillow. I flew along the dark hall, felt my way to the stair, skimming down it—another hall, another flight of stairs.

In the back passage a dim light burned. Miss Johanna's bedroom door was open a crack, and I opened it wider. In the light from behind me I could see Zoé's white shape beside the bed. Apparently she had just arrived, for Miss Johanna lay breathing heavily in deep sleep.

Zoé resisted me, but made no sound till I got her to the door. There she shouted "Let me alone!" twisting and pushing me. Still without speaking, I pulled her through the door and shut it. However, I had heard Miss Johanna's breathing stop, knew that Zoé's shout had wakened her and that she was pressing the bells beside her bed.

Before we gained the stair I heard Nannine's voice in the passage. Zoé heard it, too, came without further protest, while the commotion in the passage increased.

Up we went in the dark, saying not a word till the door of the tower room closed behind us. The big key hung in the lock. I turned it, dropped it into the pocket of my robe, lit the lamp. Zoé in her nightgown sat on the bed, her knees drawn up under her chin, her eyes brooding, her wild bright hair in a cloud about her face.

"If they had caught you," I said, speaking slowly, determined to pierce her abstraction, "I would have had to leave. I would have had to leave because you stole the key and went out. Do you want me to go?"

She answered in a monotone.

"They didn't catch me. Johanna was asleep. She sleeps like the dead. It would have been easy."

"Do you want me to go?"

The brooding eyes met mine. She shook her head, gazed at me a moment, then slid down between the sheets and went to sleep.

One hand was still knotted into a fist. I opened it and found the green string that had come around the dress boxes. It had been doubled and redoubled, twisted into a cord as big as her little finger. The sinister thing, damp from her palm, dropped to the floor and lay there like a snake. It would have been easy. Miss Johanna, lying on her back, throat bare, sleeping like the dead . . .

I picked up the cord, dropped it through the window bars.

Long after, I saw it again, woven into an oriole's nest.

134

Zoé was beyond me. I had circumvented her tonight, but, thanks to Johanna Croome, her illness would soon have progressed to a point where in Johanna's own words, she needed not a nurse but a jailer.

However, Judge Croome sent for me next day. There would be, he said, no more calls on Miss Johanna. He did not mention the disturbance of the night before. I doubt if he or anyone else suspected that Zoé had anything to do with it.

I had outwitted Ezra for once.

XV

It is perhaps a gloomy occupation to nurse a case pronounced incurable, to hope for no more than to make life endurable for the invalid till the end arrives; yet I think this is less painful than a course of keeping the patient ill lest recovery be more terrible than the disease.

I had refused at first to conform to such a plan, and I never came to share the judge's resigned acceptance of Zoé's state, nor felt that Miss Johanna's tightening of Zoé's fetters whenever they seemed to slip was less than the outcropping of a mania more pronounced than Zoé's own. To keep Zoé happy in spite of Miss Johanna, to counteract Miss Johanna's influence, these alone had become my aim, an aim easily attained after the judge forbade Zoé to visit her sister.

He looked shaken and ill the afternoon he sent for me. No doubt his interview with Miss Johanna had been upsetting. That night he had a stroke, was put to bed, and Ezra detailed to nurse him. "It's the end," Nannine said to me.

After that, Zoé went in rarely to visit him. I could imagine her sitting beside his bed, silent, since he himself could not speak. I wondered how much she noticed of his changed aspect. Apparently nothing.

There were no more dinners in the great dining room, no marshaling of the temple candlesticks, the gold service.

Miss Johanna, like her father, dined in her room.

I had blamed myself for such dangerous revival of memories as Zoé had. It was I who had "found" the dresses, taken her to the bay side, urged Belen's visit. More than one session with remorse had been mine.

I learned, however, that an even stronger influence had been at work. One morning when Stella was putting the wardrobe in order she came on a book buried under Zoé's shoes, and was about to lay it on the bed. Zoé, emerging from the bathroom, flew at her with cries and blows. As I went toward them, Stella threw the book across the room. Zoé grabbed it up, smoothed its rumpled pages, glared at Stella.

I had seen Zoé reading this book from time to time. She often read, though briefly, from the volumes on her shelves— *Quo Vadis, Trilby, Stones of Venice, Little Women, Confessions of an Opium Eater, Tom Sawyer*—a mixed assortment, surprisingly permitted by Miss Johanna, or perhaps Miss Johanna did not know.

There was nothing unusual in Zoé's reading a book, only in her hiding it. She sat now on the hassock, clasping, sheltering her treasure. When Stella had gone she came over to where I sat mending one of her dresses, and laid the book on my lap. I recognized it as the object she had taken from the old breakfront the night I came. With its tooled leather cover and silver clasp I had thought it was a box.

"Read to me," she said, as she often did, and brought the hassock and sat at my feet.

The book was a journal, a diary written in Zoé's unformed, headlong hand. The leather was crumbly, the pages with their faded ink were brittle and yellow. There was a date on the first page. June 7, 1900.

Zoé said, "I began it last year, while I was away at school . . . Why don't you start? Can't you read my writing?"

"Yes, easily."

I turned the leaves. The last entry had been made on October ninth of the same year. Most of the pages were still blank.

"Johanna doesn't know what I've written," Zoé said. "Even Skee doesn't know. Some day I'll show it to Skee."

She opened an envelope that had fallen out when Stella threw the book. Inside was a flat brown object that broke as she caressed it. "The cape jessamine," she explained, trying to piece it together again. "I wore it in my hair that first night. I'm going to keep it always." She put her nose to the fragments. "It smells sweet," she said, and held it up to me.

The smell was musty, other-world, sickening. I didn't want to read the book. I felt almost afraid of it.

Zoé was waiting. I began at the first page.

Johanna sent this book to me for a graduation gift. She writes that she can't come herself. The other girls will have families in the audience, but not me. I didn't expect Papa, but I thought Johanna would come. Not that I really care. I'm going to be frank in this diary—brutal. No one on earth is ever going to see it. I will keep it hidden as long as I live. If I find I'm going to die, I will burn it. If I die suddenly without expecting to, it will be in a place nobody knows about except me.

It's a place I saw Mama put her jewelry and some letters in. She thought I was too small to notice or remember. Anyhow, when she died I asked Papa if the old break-front might be mine, so they brought it up to my room. The letters were in it still, but not the jewelry. She had taken that out the night before she died. It was in the case on her dressing table, and in her will she left the diamonds to Johanna and the sapphires to me. I read the letters, and they were from Papa's brother who was lost at sea. I think Papa knew about him, but anyway I will never tell her secret, and I burned the letters in my fireplace, and I thought someday I will have something to put in the secret drawer myself, and I know now it will be this diary.

I wouldn't do my part in the play any better, maybe not as well, if Johanna were in the audience tomorrow. She wrote that she was too busy to come to Washington, and that I must get back in time for her big party, said she had a surprise for me. I hope and pray it's not a horse. I don't want a horse from Johanna. All I want is my beautiful white Selim that she crippled and had shot. I mustn't think about Selim. Everything goes red before my eyes.

I must go to Hall and rehearse *Midsummer Night's Dream*.

"Did I tell you about Selim?" Zoé whispered to me. She sat upright, a wild light in her eyes.

"Yes," I answered, though it was Belen who had told me. "What about the play?"

139

She settled down again.

"I was Puck. We gave it at Commencement. I didn't write about it, didn't have time. I was going to write on the way home, but I met a boy from Baltimore on the train, and I didn't have time. I promised to write to him—see, there's his address—but I don't intend to, now that Skee . . . Skip a little. That's just about the trip. Skip to here."

She laid her head on my knee.

June 12. I got home this morning. Ezra met me because Papa is out of town. He probably won't be here for the ball tonight. Men were hanging fairy lanterns in the trees and along the verandas when I reached the house. I felt happy and thrilled as if something wonderful was going to happen. I'm glad I got home in time. It certainly is a surprise—this party—all because I've come home. I didn't know Johanna cared about me at all, and it's been a long time since I've cared about her. But right now I'm happy. I feel like a bird or a bear or something just let out of a cage.

Ezra stopped the carriage in the porte-cochère, and a young man I didn't know came out and said, "I'm Schuyler Winn." I smiled back and said, "I'm Zoé." He said, "Yes, I know. But you don't look a bit like your sister."

Handsome and tall. His voice sounds as if he sings. Might be a baritone. If I see him again I'm going to ask him. I like men's voices. The house is full of flowers, and floors have been laid for dancing in the big double parlors and in the music room, and a dais is at the end of the north parlor for the musicians to sit on. Johanna's debut party was in the old banquet room, but I think she's right

—June is no time to ask people to climb two flights of stairs.

All the servants came to greet me—Jessie and Reba, Dink and Dan'l and Belen. They were busy as bees, and Johanna came down the stair smiling, and kissed me, and said to the young man—Schuyler Winn— "How do you like my little sister?" He smiled, too, as if he were embarrassed, or too shy to pay me a compliment. Johanna said, "He thinks you're lovely. Now run upstairs and get a bath and a nap for tonight."

It's good to be in my own room again. My silver clock and crystal vases. My desk in the old breakfront, my books and my bed. How I've missed them! How I've missed the sea! . . . I thought when I went away I didn't care if I never saw them again. I was so miserable over Selim. But I didn't like going back to school—even a finishing school —either, when I thought I was through with education, though I guess it was a good idea. You can't know too much.

I bought lots of pretty clothes with the check Papa sent me for my graduation. Jessie has been unpacking my trunk, putting them away, exclaiming over them. I gave her her present, a white shirtwaist with red buttons. She was so pleased. I gave them all their presents.

Well, now I know. Schuyler Winn and Johanna are going to be married. That's what the ball is about. Wasn't I silly, thinking it was for me? I ran into Johanna in the back passage and she told me. I said, "Why didn't you write me about it?" She said, "Because I wanted to surprise you." And she laughed because she had. She said that when she announced it tonight everybody else would be surprised too. Of course they will. Nobody has ever believed Johanna would take a husband. She wouldn't respect a man she could boss, and she wouldn't marry one she couldn't. Schuyler must have struck the happy balance or whatever it would be. I'd hate to see anyone kick him around. He seems so sensitive for a man, so quiet and proud.

It's funny, but I can't associate him with Johanna at all. She looks older than he does, but she's regal and beautiful, and she's really in love. I talked with Schuyler at lunch. He came to Muspa six months ago to teach the violin. He's doing all right, but Johanna says he's a genius and she has greater plans for him. They'll travel, for one thing, visit all the great capitals, hear all the great music. She shut the door of the music room and made him play for me while she accompanied him on the piano.

The violin has a soul. It truly has a soul. I never realized.

"Olive," said Zoé in a low voice. "What you are thinking is not true."

"I'm not thinking, Zoé. I'm just reading."

"All right. Read on."

Johanna's been in and decided on the dress I'm to wear tonight. Turquoise blue organdie. It's pretty, but I did want to wear the rose-pink chiffon with the diamanté, because it floats when I dance. Johanna said pink would never go with her yellow.

She was sweet and sentimental, and talked about the time we used to ride with our governess in the pony cart all over Yonder (we *were* good friends in those days) and onto the ferry and into Muspa to get Nelly Dane—only Johanna says she calls herself Helen now that she's married to Roger Carrington. Roger's always been so dignified, I wonder what she wanted with *him*. Nell was such fun, ready for anything, even back in those days Johanna was talking about, when Mama was alive, and everybody was happy—only maybe Mama *wasn't* happy, but we thought she was.

Johanna says Roger's taking Nell away to some place where there's more business than there is in Muspa. Well, I'll see her tonight. And it's nice to find Johanna so sweet. She talked about Schuyler and said, "He's all I want in the world." And she kissed me.

I wonder if I'll keep on writing in this diary.

Everybody was surprised, and the dance made a real splash. Johanna's pale yellow net was embroidered in dark gold flowers. She looked like a queen with her black hair piled up into a crown.

I went downstairs early because she had asked me to fix the dance programmes. They're very pretty with the gilt letters J and S entwined on them, but their pencil cords had got all tangled.

My blue organdie looked lovely after Reba pressed it. It's that new silk organdie, and the skirt stands out all around, and I wore silver slippers, and Reba did my hair. She said it was more golden than ever, and that I looked like an angel.

I could hear the orchestra tuning up as I went down.

Jessie and Dink were lighting the candles. The music made little shivers go through me, the way music does. I felt so happy I knew I could float if I tried. I started to try, there on the stair, held out my arms and was going to float down, but I saw Schuyler in the hall watching me, and I came down the ordinary way.

He had the dance programmes and we went into the den and sat down on the sofa and began to work with the strings. He looked wonderful in his white suit. He has dark eyes, but they're really blue. And he doesn't talk unless he wants to. I realized he hadn't been embarrassed when Johanna asked him what he thought of me, nor too shy to pay me a compliment. He just preferred to be silent.

The pencils were a nuisance, getting themselves all snarled up like that. Schuyler was patient with them, and careful. I stopped jerking at the knots and let him do the job. Pretty soon he had them straightened out, and we put them in stacks on a wide silver tray. I said, "Let's try the floor," for the sounds the musicians were making drove me wild.

People were beginning to come. I could hear them in the hall, men and girls being directed to their separate dressing rooms off the bay-side veranda. We slipped into the parlors and had things all to ourselves, with the orchestra playing *Over the Waves*. I love that waltz, and I liked dancing with him, the way he held me, and the way our steps seemed to go together.

Is he really going to be my brother? I'll tell him all my troubles. Why do I want to tell things? I told them to my roommate, and they got out all over school, and I knew she had betrayed me. She got jealous because I was voted

144

the prettiest girl in school, and she was only the most intellectual . . . And I tell them to this diary which *can't* betray me unless I leave it lying around which I never will. And now I want to tell things to Schuyler. I think it's because I'm so full, like a corked-up bottle with something fermenting inside, for I've never been able to tell things to Johanna. Only I wish Schuyler would talk to me more. He talks to Johanna and to Papa. Everybody calls him Skee.

Papa came home during the dance. He took me back into his study, wanted to see me alone after all these months, to see if I was really "finished" after the school in Washington. Papa must have his little joke. Said, at any rate, I had grown. Grown, when I'm twenty. I suppose that's young to him.

What fun! None of the boys knew I'd come home, and they gave me a rush. There weren't extras enough. My programme's a sight. Nell—Helen, that is—hadn't expected me either. She had on a dress the color of a tea rose, and she looked lovely, the old red-head. Roger's not bad-looking, either, but so dignified. You sort of want to stick a pin in him to deflate him. I'll bet Nell leads him a dance.

Papa announced Johanna's engagement at supper, and seemed pleased and happy for her. Johanna sat beside Schuyler. She shone like the candles. Schuyler shone, too, in his quiet way. Johanna's leaving for New York to buy her trousseau. I've always wanted to go to New York. I think she might let me. She says I've been away long enough. She says it's my turn to look after Papa.

XVI

Zoé snatched the book away.

"You're blaming me, Olive. I knew it. You're blaming me for taking Skee away from Johanna. I can tell by your voice."

"Did you take him away, Zoé?"

"No! He was mine from the start. He says it was like the tide coming in. Yes," kneeling upright, closing her eyes, "it's like that. It's like being on Lonely, and the tide coming in on every side. Who can stop it? . . . I don't want you to read any more if you blame me. I won't give him up. Don't tell me to. It's too late."

"I understand."

"And even if I gave him up, he won't marry Johanna. Not now. He wants to tell her about us, and I won't let him. I know her too well. She never dreamed that anyone could take him away. I wanted to go with her to New York, and she wouldn't let me. And the morning she went—the morning she took the ferry—I felt sick and unhappy. I thought it was because she was leaving me behind when I wanted so to go. But it was different from that, the feeling I had. I felt—I felt afraid.

"Now if I'd been meaning to take Skee away, I wouldn't have been unhappy at her going. *You* know that. I'd have been glad. We'd never been alone, Skee and I, never tried to be. But we did like dancing together, and when he played the violin it was like nothing I'd ever felt on earth.

"That first time we met alone was almost an accident. It was down on the bay side the day after Johanna left. I keep *Gypsy*, my little naphtha launch, tied there, and I was going into Muspa to a garden party. And there, coming from the pier, was Skee, with the beautiful pale blue parrot he was bringing for Johanna, wanting to surprise her when she came home. He said he could take me into the village if I would wait till he carried in the parrot. I walked back to the house with him, and the parrot kept calling out, 'I love my wife, but oh you kid!'

"We couldn't help laughing, and then we met Ezra, and Skee gave him the parrot and told him to hang the cage in Johanna's room, and we went to Muspa in a little sailboat, *La Brisa*, that belongs to Skee's roommate who plays the saxophone, and has gone to Havana where he has an orchestra. His name is Juan Moreno—John Brown. Skee went to the party with me. It was a Sunday afternoon. I had on my pink dotted swiss.

"That was the beginning. After that I saw *La Brisa* nearly every day—from the beach or the bay side. And I would wave to Skee, and he would land or take me for a sail. At first it was fun. Sometimes we stopped at the Mirada pier and danced.

"One evening, coming back from the Mirada, he gave me my watch. It had been his mother's. His father had given it to her when they married. And now Skee gave it to me instead of to Johanna. He said, 'I want you to have it.'

"It made me cry.

"I said, 'I love you, but you know.'

"He took me in his arms, and I said, 'What are we going to do?'

"He said, 'We'll tell Johanna. She'll understand.'

"He doesn't know Johanna at all. She impresses people as generous and broad-minded. But I thought about Selim. She tried to break his spirit, to make him mind her when he hated her, and she couldn't, and she had him shot. I thought about how he had bled when she whipped him, of how she had crippled him . . . I thought how she'd be coming back with her trousseau, ready to be married, and how she had said that Skee was all she wanted on earth. I couldn't let him tell her that he wasn't going to marry her, that he loved me. It may be the right thing, it may be taking your stand—that's what Skee calls it anyhow. Well, Selim took his stand.

"I can't bear to think about Selim," covering her face. "I can't bear to think about Skee facing Johanna. We've got to run away."

She clasped and unclasped her hands, staring before her.

"One day we went to Lonely Key. I knew we'd have the beach to ourselves on Lonely, and we didn't have to hurry home because Papa had gone to St. Augustine, and nobody would know how late we stayed.

"Last year some people from up north built a little lodge on Lonely to come down to in the winter and loaf and fish.

We found it when it began to rain, one of those quick summer rains that don't come down in drops but in bucketfuls. It was dark in there at first, because it's in the very middle of the jungle, and then the rain too . . . But we found a stub of candle in the kitchen and lit it, and sat there on the bunk in each other's arms. And the rain beat and beat on the roof, and I had a feeling that I was never going to see Skee after that day, and the candle burned itself out, and Skee kissed me and said my name over and over, and there was nothing in the world but Skee.

"I didn't know. I didn't know what love does, how it takes you and shakes you as if you had no will at all, and how there are deeps and deeps of love. It would be easy to die of love, to drown. I drowned in Skee's arms that night. I'll die—I'll drown myself really if anything robs me of Skee. He knows that I will. I've told him so. But nothing can part us now. That was what he answered. Nothing must come between us now.

"It was almost dawn when we made our way down the path to the boat. We had been there all night. The rain had stopped. It was still dark, but there was a light in the east. The water was black and quiet. We sat together at the tiller, and Skee's arm was around me close. Oh, I was glad we weren't going to wait for Johanna to come home, glad when Skee said we were going to run away.

"The sun was coming up when we reached our pier, and I saw that the *Gypsy* wasn't tied at the place I had tied her when Skee and I slipped away. That worried me. Where had she been, and who had dared take her while I was gone?

"Skee said it didn't matter, since whoever had taken her

had brought her back. He was thinking about all that had to be done, all the arrangements he must make to get away. He said, 'I'll see you tonight,' and he came with me through the grove. I felt as if someone was following us, someone noiseless as a panther. I was frightened, but Skee said it was nothing, some little wood animal hunting his breakfast. We got to the house without seeing anybody, but I was afraid for Skee to go back through the grove, and he laughed at me, and said I could watch from a window and see him come out on the bay and know the bears hadn't got him. And I did. I went into Mama's old room and watched, and the *Brisa* came out in the dawn, and Skee blinked his little light.

"That was yesterday, and in the afternoon Johanna came home ahead of time, and in the evening Papa came too. *And Johanna knew.* She knew that Skee and I had been seeing each other. She even knew that we had been all night together on Lonely Key. Oh what terrible things she said, most of them true. And Papa was there. He looked as if he wouldn't or couldn't believe. But she made him. Oh it was awful that Papa was there. I felt crushed before him, before his face, his words—not many words, but terrible. I wanted to hide myself. I wanted to hide myself in Skee. But Skee wasn't there, and I didn't want him there . . . How had Johanna found out? Who had spied on us? Who had followed us, even to Lonely Key, and back into the jungle?

"One of the servants, perhaps—but why? I've been good to them all and they like me . . . I had on my watch when Johanna came back so unexpectedly. I hadn't meant her to see it, but she spied it right away, and asked me where I got it. I said I bought it—while I was away. She looked at it close while my heart beat hard. 'You gave a pretty penny for it,' she said. But she believed me. She would smash it or burn it if she knew Skee gave it to me.

"Anyway, by evening I was standing in her room, and Papa was there, and Johanna knew everything. Not about the watch, but everything that Skee and I thought was our own secret. All the time she was talking, accusing me, calling me names—thief and slut and she-devil, and names I won't repeat because they're not true—all the time she was saying these things, the parrot Skee had given her was making his silly joke about 'Oh you kid,' sitting on his perch outside his cage, moving sideways, cocking his head. He looked as if he were kidding Johanna, making fun of her.

"All of a sudden she picked up a shoe—one of the new trousseau shoes—and struck him a blow with the heel. He dropped to the floor and lay there twitching a little, with his head bleeding, then he was still, just a lump of blue feathers.

And I heard myself screaming because—because he had been alive a minute before, and because Skee had brought him. And I ran to my room and locked the door, and walked up and down, crying. And I heard Johanna still talking to Papa in the hall, and later she came and tried my door, but it was locked. She shook it, but it was locked.

"Nobody said a word at dinner, and my face was all swollen from crying, and later when I went up to my room the key to my door was gone. I can't find it anywhere. I know Johanna has taken it, so I can't lock myself in. What does she think she's going to do?

"Anyhow, last night I slipped out to Skee and met him in the grove, and he told me his plans. We're leaving today in

151

the *Brisa,* joining Juan Moreno in Havana. We'll be married there. Skee's going to play in Juan's orchestra.

"He hadn't been home all day, so I know any message Johanna had sent hadn't reached him. I didn't tell him she was home. I didn't want him seeing her or Papa. We talked in whispers because I still felt as if something was listening, and once there was a sound like a twig breaking. But nobody could hear what we said because we whispered and could hardly hear each other.

"Skee came with me to the edge of the grove, and then he went back. And I heard—I thought I heard voices in the grove. I ran back, and—" A troubled look. "I . . . ran . . . back. No, I . . . don't know."

Her face cleared.

"Skee has managed everything," she said. "This is the day.

"I've told you all I can't put in the book. I must go now. Skee will be watching for me. On the bay side, or if I'm not there, down by the jetty on the beach. Johanna can't see the bay from her room, and while she can see the beach, she can't see the jetty. Come on, Olive—please."

"What shall I do with the book?"

"Keep it for me. Johanna has my key. How do I know she won't search my room? How do I know she won't find the secret drawer? Some day I'll come back and get all my things. Papa will forgive me."

I locked the book in a drawer in my room.

She never spoke of it again.

She had dressed herself with unusual care, the watch, which she wound so faithfully, pinned in place. As we left the drive she picked a sprig of the white Madeira flower and fastened it in her hair. There was the usual plea to go to the bay side, the customary petulance at refusal, the forgetting of the argument, the urgent flying to the palm trees. I noticed this morning that the palms concealed her from the house, and, as often before, I observed how surreptitious she became when we passed the door of a bedroom on the second floor. This I knew had been Johanna's room till she grew too disabled to climb the stair. This was the room where they had quarreled about Skee, where the parrot had been killed.

"Johanna sleeps till noon when she's been to a party," Zoé told me once. "But I can't be sure."

That day while she kept her vigil Richard joined me beside the cabaña. Would I like to drudge on my afternoons off, he wanted to know. The lady to whom he took his final typing had broken her wrist, and while he could find somebody else if he looked around . . .

"I'll be glad to," I said.

How did he know I could type? I must have dropped the boast at some time.

It was, it seemed, a commercial proposition, and when I said that I was not a professional and typed only for love, he replied firmly that then he must look around.

"Oh, very well, but you've stifled a noble impulse."

That was my free afternoon, and he asked me to come directly after lunch.

We walked down to where Zoé sat, and seeing Richard, she came with us in silence. On the way home he found a pheasant shell, spiral and tapering, brilliantly tinted. He dropped it into her hand, and she fingered and turned it, saying nothing.

After lunch when Nannine had come I went to Richard's house, taking the shorter way through the grove . . . What had happened here, I wondered? What ghosts were in this place? Zoé remembered only the rustle in the grass, the creeping step, the feeling that someone was listening, so that they talked in whispers, making their plans for tomorrow. All around them the ferns and moss, the coiling vines with their blood-red blossoms. Feeling their way, meeting breathlessly, whispering, locked in each other's arms . . . The grove was not terrible then. There were no ghosts, only the soft step of someone creeping . . .

Why did they not go that night? Was it that he wanted to come openly in the sunlight, a lover taking what was his own? Or was there something still to be done before he could leave? . . . What had happened? What had happened that last night that Zoé and Skee had met, the night that time had stopped for her?

Richard was waiting for me. He had placed the big typewriter on a desk in the jalousied breezeway, parts of his roughly typed script beside it. He helped me to get settled in what is known as a posture chair. Did I like it? I did. Was it the right height for the desk? Precisely.

"And you'll get a breeze from the sea in a little while."

He went back to his portable and the throes of composition.

His notes and interlineations were legible, and no need came to disturb him. I clicked away with Rory lounging at my feet or sitting outside the door of the study where Richard had shut himself away. At half-past three Richard looked into the breezeway to say "Coffee break," and Floyd brought the steaming pot and a plate of sandwiches into the living room.

To go to Richard's house was almost to enter the world again. In the world it would have been equally an oasis, a place where you could say what you pleased, certain of being understood. I think everyone interested Richard. When he talked during that coffee break it was generally of the people he had known. He seldom spoke of his journeys. You had to read his books to know where he had been. It was *Kattegat* he was writing then, but it was not of the Kattegat he talked.

There was the girl he had married. Yes, he had been married, was that surprising?

"Only because I didn't know."

"Yet I knew about you. Perhaps my marriage didn't leave so deep an impression as yours, not lasting so long."

"I have not been married," I remarked. "But I know what you mean. Tell me about your wife."

"Well, she was new in town. Secretary to a lawyer when I married her. Name's Marcia. She thought she wouldn't mind having an explorer for a husband. Inside a year she knew better."

"Where is she now?"

"Down the coast. She married again, has twin boys. Her husband's an inventor, a dreamer, but he stays home. She does my typing."

155

"And she's broken her wrist."

"Yes, a bad break. I sent Dr. Gordon from Muspa to look at it."

He had sent Dr. Gordon. I suspected that he did many things for Marcia, her twins and her husband. Did it mean that he still cared? Or did it mean that his feeling for her had slipped painlessly into friendship? . . . Had Marcia lived on Yonder? I wondered. Was that her posture chair?

He said as if answering me, "It happened before I came here, close to six years ago. Marcia would not have liked Yonder any more than she liked being married to a traveling man. My mother warned me that Marcia would be unhappy, and yet she wanted me to marry, encouraged the idea all she could."

"She thought Marcia would keep you home."

He smiled, told me something of his mother who, as a young invalid, had married her doctor, and after ten years borne him a son. Hadn't wanted that son to join the Navy since he was under draft age, but he was restless, and besides he felt comfortable in uniform, being tall, and looking older than he was. She had said when he left, "I shall never see you again."

Yet she had been there when he came back.

"I stayed alive to pray for you," she told him.

Now he no longer needed her prayers, and she was tired of pain. She was willing to go, and so she went.

Marcia. I could not visualize her from his meager description. Certainly I could not see her as the woman I had pictured "down the coast." . . . Had she known her inventor a long time, or had they met while Richard was away? He

156

appeared to have been standing there, waiting, when Richard let her go. Somehow they had kept his good will.

I wanted him to talk more about Marcia, but when the sandwiches gave out we went back to our desks.

Except on Thursdays Zoé came with me while I typed the book. She made no trouble, busying herself with the crayons Richard kept for her, or decking herself in trophies of his travels—a necklace of sharks' teeth, bracelets of sweet-smelling nuts, a crown of waving feathers, earrings of pearls and shells. There were island cosmetics that made her look startling indeed, and curious pipes and walking sticks. A pig-sticker and a tom-tom Richard had wisely put away.

I remember a kaleidoscope that Zoé played with at Richard's house. It kept her amused by the hour, and no wonder. She called me sometimes to look at the patterns the bits of colored glass fell into. For me or for Richard that oldest of toys came up with conventional designs, but when Zoé touched it an imp of mischief woke inside. Once she showed me rings of green monkeys, and once a circle of skulls and roses. Sometimes she would laugh to herself, shielding it with her hand, shutting us out. She never disturbed us, never spoke except during the coffee break at half-past three.

In those days I came to know that her love for Richard was the love of a child for its father. I knew that love, and saw it in her eyes as I had not seen it when she was with the judge. Richard's behavior was that of a father, in turn. I am sure he never reminded himself that she was older than he by many years, but accepted her as the perennial child.

More than once, watching them, I longed to be his child.

The evening the book was finished I walked home by way of the lime grove. The road led past the kitchens of Yonder where I had sometimes caught sight of the swarthy, Spanish-looking cook in his high white cap; past the stables that were garages now, past barns and chicken runs, laundry and drying yard, past incinerator and power plant. Leaving these, the road became a path leading into the lime grove, then out of its shadows and suddenly to the bay.

I think it was the contrast—in scene and odors—that drew me home by this route whenever I was alone.

Today the sun had gone out of the water. Bay and sky were moon-colored without any moon. The boat lights glimmered mistily, and there was stillness everywhere, a feeling of enchantment and transience, as if all might vanish in an instant like a bubble.

A light fell on the castle. A strange light. I saw for the first time a row of stained-glass windows, Gothic windows, wine-red and violet and iris-blue, burning as if there were a light behind them. Chapel windows. This was the west wing, I reminded myself, the bay side. Some day I must go all through Croome Castle, must find the chapel, the banquet hall, the dungeon, if it had one . . . I stood looking at the windows, burning more richly as the twilight darkened.

A feeling of dread came over me, a sense of apprehension, as if a dark wing had brushed me. Once before I had known this darkening of the spirit, this foreboding. When? . . . The night of the picnic, a thousand years ago, the night of the fireworks. Andrew had said, "If you give way to things like that—"

A chuckle sounded beside me. I knew that it was an owl.

In my own state he would have hooted, here he laughed. Again the sound, low and mischievous, a double chuckle. Then a flap of black wings out of a black tree. He was gone.

I walked on through gardens full of evening fragrance, past the figure of a young faun playing his pipes, then up a flight of stone steps set with marble vases of geraniums.

On the terrace I saw the ocean and the evening star.

In the tower room Nannine sat by a window crocheting an eternal bedspread. Zoé was playing the phonograph—Drdla's *Souvenir*—a muted melody with a click in it. The enchantment of the evening lay over them like a veil.

"Hello!" Nannine said, and the spell was broken.

She looked at her watch, told me the time. I might have lingered by the bay a little longer.

When she had gone Zoé produced a letter.

"Ezra brought it," she whispered. All letters were clandestine with Zoé, things to be dealt with darkly.

This one was from Helen Carrington. For some reason I stood with it in my hand, wanting not to open it, wanting to give it back to Zoé and let her return it to the secret pocket in her skirt. There was news in it—what? Perhaps only that one of the Carringtons was coming to Yonder, I thought, and broke the seal.

". . . and if you are not happy there I want you to leave."

That was near the end, the first words my glance fell on as I took the letter out. I turned to the beginning.

Leonie was dead. Leonie, Dane's wife, had given premature birth to a girl, and died. She had been gone nearly a week.

They had just moved into their new house . . . Hard on her parents. Dane seems lost. We are going to take the baby. The Roys are away so much.

I am writing Johanna also, since I owe her a letter. . . . I'd like to say this to you, now that you've had a change in scene and climate—we want you to come back and live with us. I wanted it when you left, but I felt you needed to get away. Johanna has been reticent about you, and if you're not happy there I want you to leave.

With love,
Helen Carrington

P.S. Try to come in time for Christmas.

I stood thinking of Leonie. Leonie with her long eyelids and frail bird-bones, her angular ballerina movements, her soft appeal that made slaves of her friends. Leonie, broken under the one burden she was forced to bear alone. She had lain in Dane's arms, she had borne him a child, and she was dead . . .

Was there some dark triumph in my heart? Could any mortal rejoice in the death of another when we all stand beside the same intangible curtain that may so easily, so instantly part for us and close again? . . . Dane's freedom could mean nothing to me. "Dane seems lost." He would find himself again, in his own world which he had never really left. That shining figure clouded for a while by absorption in another, would emerge from its eclipse, brighter perhaps than ever. But the thought of Dane stunned even for an hour by grief was strange and terrible.

Leonie. Had her parents no other child? Yes, there was a boy, a younger brother, who came out to St. Hilda's to see

Leonie on Saturdays, to take her to pictures or games. He wore the uniform of some military school, and he had his sister's slenderness and dark eyes. I remembered their walking together in the grounds, looking lonely, orphaned almost, with their parents in Europe . . . A boy would not take the place of a girl. But there was Leonie's daughter. . . . Dane had his daughter.

"Is it bad?" asked Zoé, watching me.

Drdla's *Souvenir,* which was always to suggest Leonie to me, was still going round, its click almost as frequent as the tick of a clock. Zoé came and stood beside me.

"What is it?" she asked.

I told her that a friend had died, leaving her newborn child. Zoé's limpid, sea-colored eyes were fathomless in their sympathy.

"You asked me once," I said, "if I had ever had a lover. I told you he had married someone else. The girl who died, the mother of the child, was his wife."

I saw that she did not remember.

When the wise man said, "Know thyself," he was thinking, no doubt, of the abyss from which our motives rise. Could we know why we do this instead of that, we would be in a fair way of knowing ourselves.

What obscure reasoning kept me on Yonder, marooned me on this island, imprisoned me in a house where the malign presence of Johanna Croome could be felt the moment I began to descend the stair; where the shadowy Ezra, like some emanation from herself, prowled noiselessly, seeming to see all, hear all; and where the racked body of Judge Croome in the bedroom next to Miss Johanna's grew daily more helpless and emaciated.

I wrote Helen Carrington that I had become attached to Zoé, and that I had promised her to stay. I did not write that I was also attached to Yonder, that I tasted the actual essence of happiness when I wandered the key with Richard, or sat typing his book, or poured his coffee, talking with him, or perhaps silent. I would not acknowledge this happiness or touch it with a possessive hand. I was afraid, as if it were some shining crystal bowl, carried perilously. Nothing seemed secure.

Often words that Dane had said, light words embedded in my mind, rose to the surface to contradict or deride. There was his recipe for keeping a friend—to make no confidences and to ask no favors.

I had replied, of course, that a friend was not a friend unless you could confide in him, and ask and grant favors. He smiled, that being precisely what he had meant. There are no friends. "I never made a confidence," he said, "that I didn't regret."

"Even in me, Dane?"

"Oh, you . . ." he said, as if that were different.

I had confided in Richard about Dane himself. I had felt better afterward, but had it been wise? Had it been wise also to tell him about Leonie's death, and that Mrs. Carrington had asked me to come back and live in her home?

"You'll go, of course," he said.

"No, I've written her that I won't."

He nodded. "I hope she doesn't take you seriously."

But she had.

"Somehow," she wrote, "I feel that I should make you come. It will soon be a year since you left. I never dreamed you would stay longer than that. Lately I've had a premonition about you, Olive, about Yonder. It probably amounts to nothing, but I am not given to such things . . ."

She enclosed a picture of Dane's daughter who looked much like any other baby of six weeks but who bore the unusual name of Dorilys. Zoé, coming in on me as I read the letter, fancied the picture of Dorilys, kept it in her hand and would not give it back. I found it afterward among her shells and returned it to my locked desk.

XVII

Christmas drew near on a quickened tide of flowers and sunshine. I took Zoé's list and mine and did a day's shopping in Muspa. Later the two of us found branches of Florida holly whose red berries the robins had spared and decorated the tower room. On Christmas Eve we went to Richard's house for dinner.

The gloom in Croome Castle seemed to have deepened as we passed through the halls. No wreath, no candle, no sense of preparation anywhere. Miss Johanna, Nannine had told me, never noticed Christmas, but the old man always gave presents of money to the help, indoors and out, and had signified that the custom be maintained this year.

The sunlight seemed the more dazzling as we went outside, taking the beach road, arriving with our presents at Richard's house. Here, too, were garlands of holly, and in the center of the table a small yew tree decked in silver and tapers and little gifts. There was a turkey that Floyd had stuffed with oysters, and there were cranberries and asparagus and wild rice and coconut ice cream. Rory had on a red collar.

After dinner we all went for a sail in the *Chantey*, tied now at the pier, waiting for her journey to Damballa Oueddo. Her bottom had been scraped, her hull repainted; she had a new set of sails, a new auxiliary engine. Richard took us over her, galley and locker room, forecastle and cabin, while the well-balanced boat sailed a straight course alone. I saw the extra bunk forward, used now for storing ropes and sails. I thought of my dream.

"The *Chantey* seems small," I said.

A cockleshell when I thought of the Atlantic. But crossing an ocean, he informed me, was simpler than coastal sailing if you knew your job. And I knew that he had made longer journeys than this in his one-man *Chantey*.

On New Year's Day we helped him stock the larder. Pemmican, milk in cans and in tablets, tropical chocolate bars. Also aboard went camera, radio and typewriter, and a hundred other things, including provisions in case of shipwreck —luminous distress flags, storm oil, self-igniting water lights. Books went, too, a few of fiction, more of biography, more still of poetry. Like some other mariners, he had found poetry to be more seaworthy than prose, liked to shout it aloud, he said, on long evenings at the tiller. *How They Brought the Good News from Ghent to Aix. The Battle of Ivry. The Road to Mandalay.*

"One night I had a whale following me, listening."

Packing the books, I ran across a snapshot marking the place in Yeats—me sitting on a reef with my arm around Cato, the pelican. Me in shorts, marking a poem, "When you are old and gray and full of sleep . . ."

"Talisman," explained Richard. He added, "I wonder if all will be the same when I come back."

"We'll see," remarked Zoé, storing cans of instant coffee.

"That's it," said Richard. "We'll see."

He sailed one day at dawn. I locked the door of the tower room and came through the grove to see him go. The dew was heavy and the world in twilight except for a veiled glimmer in the east. We stood hand-in-hand on the pier, for Floyd had told me that it would bring bad luck if a woman went on board at sailing time. Richard laughed at the warning, but I wouldn't go.

We kissed good-by. It was a bitter kiss. Not to Richard, perhaps. This was his work. He was not afraid of the sea.

I would not watch him go. I closed my eyes, unwilling to see the boat become a star and vanish like that other boat . . . No, I must watch him round the key, enter the ocean . . . There he was at the tiller, waving his hand.

The boat did not become a star, but a gray bird, winging darkly into the mist.

XVIII

There were no seasons on Yonder. Only the birds knew, only the Winter People. Glittering days darkened into cool blowing nights, and came again. The ceaseless breeding sun, the millions of stars . . . Then one day you went into Muspa and the Winter People were gone. Shuffleboard courts deserted, awning umbrellas vanished from the beaches, sails fewer on the bay. We were alone with the gulls and the sudden bright gushes of rain, alone with those birds that never left us.

More than once during the time of the Winter People I had felt an alien to this warmth and perfume, to the idle, fondling breeze, and the flames of bougainvillea; times when I longed for icy rain in my face, for the crunch of snow underfoot, and the bare black branches of trees against a red sunset; for tart apples and for twilights that smelled of woodsmoke, for the long gray stretch of winter that made the first bluebird a miracle.

I asked Zoé once if she had ever heard sleighbells, and she said yes, last year in Washington, at school. She had gone sleighing, and the snow was piled over everything, a white city. "A white city," she repeated dreamily.

I went into Muspa and bought me a dress. Red. The red I had never owned. The salesgirl said, "This is your color—your dress." It was my dress. A sheer fabric, sleeveless, exquisitely cut. A rounded neckline that would look well with the strand of cultured pearls Helen Carrington had sent me at Christmas.

I wore it for Zoé at dinner. She appreciated it.

For a month after Richard went she had expected him back every day. He had given us his key that I might use his library when I liked. It was Zoé who daily, after her vigil, insisted on going to Richard's house, gathering flowers along the beach road, removing the faded ones of the day before, dusting, sweeping, smoothing his bed. It was good to see her diverted so harmlessly, and Rory, whom we always found on the porch, though he was supposed to stay with Floyd, was glad to see us. Now and then her preparations were so realistic—as when she once undertook to prepare Richard's dinner—that I came myself to hope he would raise our island by nightfall.

His letters read like a sailor's log.

"Passed through snow and rain last night. Wind W to NW to N. High waves. *Chantey* lying fine . . . Sleet. Deck slippery with ice." Or, "Brilliant sun and sea. Expect to raise Nassau by noon." "Last night got out the volume of Masefield that Olive gave me Christmas and read to the sky. Fine clear sky with an old moon. Once Olive said she wanted to come with me, but backed down. Last night I thought she was aboard. Just a dream, of course, but there she sat, beside me at the tiller, real as the moon . . . Small ESE breeze, shifting to N. Lively enough to fill sails."

He wrote no letters naturally after reaching his island. Chances of communicating with him were as remote as if he had landed on Jupiter. Perhaps he had *not* landed—how were we to know? The radio, getting wind of his travels, spoke of Damballa Oueddo as a cannibal island, a description that did not add to my peace of mind.

In the months that followed I tried to imagine Richard forever cruising, seeking and not finding his goal. I knew, however, that in that case he might have mailed a letter.

At last the log began again as he turned toward home . . . Weather. The sturdiness and gallantry of the *Chantey*. Snow. Snow in June. I read the letters to Zoé. "Radio's on the blink," he wrote.

Then came the day our own radio shouted warnings, and the red and black hurricane flags were flying on the mainland. The sea gulls had been circling and screaming since dawn.

Richard's last letter had been mailed on Martinique. He was by now in the Caribbean, that breeder of hurricanes, blue as a baby's eyes, I had once been told.

No mariner, I assured myself, puts out into a hurricane. But they came so suddenly there. Here, we have our warnings, but there at the source—was there time? I thought of all the tales of shipwreck I had ever read. I thought of the distress flags that he had known he might need, of the storm oil and water lights; of the cockleshell and the great ocean. I thought of my dream, of Helen Carrington's premonition.

Zoé knelt beside me, listening to the radio.

"Richard will come and see that we are all right," she prattled, forgetting that he was gone. "We'll ask him to stay. You won't be afraid if Richard is with us."

So she knew that I was afraid.

We looked our last from the windows before Ezra came to seal them. Our familiar world of sunshine and laughing waters was gone. Black skies hung over a black-green ocean that seemed to breathe heavily. The gulls had disappeared, and there was stillness and a rank smell of seaweed. A sullen, a menacing world.

Ezra clamped on the heavy cypress blinds, fastened the inside shutters. The rooms grew hot and dark. I lit candles, watching Ezra and his shadow move from window to window. Zoé sat swaying to music she had found on the radio.

"Ezra," she said when he had finished, "go tell Mr. Lowrie to come to us. Tell him to come and see that we are all right."

"Mr. Lowrie is not here," replied Ezra. "He is in the Bahamas."

"Did you hear that?" she said to me when Ezra had gone. "Richard's out in the hurricane."

"He'll find shelter," I said.

"His radio's on the blink," she answered with that uncanny trick of culling from the echoes in her mind the most disturbing sound.

"It's fixed now," I told her. "He's made port more than once since then."

The rain we had been having for days began again and there was a sound of heaving seas. Static like crackling fire broke from the radio, rose to a shrieking of banshees. The thread of music came, too, and as I lit the lamp, Zoé danced.

170

She had on a light green muslin and its soft skirt floated around her. Her hair floated, too, as she moved with shining eyes, one with the fire and the banshees. The door was open by Ezra's direction to keep the pressure equalized, so I must watch Zoé.

That morning and the day before she had made no preparation for her vigil on the beach. I had waited, expecting her to say that Skee would not mind the rain. Many times in raincoats and even in bathing suits, liking the adventure, we had gone along the beach in the rain, but now for three days, all during the hurricane warnings, she had laid the custom aside, had seemed to forget.

There came a sound from inside the house. A cry.

"What's that?" I asked, nervous as a witch. "Turn off the radio."

Zoé seemed to come back from far away. I listened, heard the sound again, realized that it was the dumb-waiter, that we must eat even with the hurricane close at hand.

I went into the hall, brought in our food, belatedly set the table. All through supper Zoé hummed the tune that had been on the radio.

A whispering began outside our blinds, a vast susurrus, above the churning of the waves, the pounding of the rain. The murmur that lived on Yonder rose into a moan, into a universal howl. And now the wind hurled itself upon the house as if to tear it away while overhead the million banshees shrieked and screamed.

I carried the dishes back to the dumb-waiter, rang, watched it descend. It was good to know that there were other people in the house. The servants would wash the dishes now, go to their wing . . . What was Miss Johanna doing? Judge Croome? Waiting stoically, certain that their fortress was impregnable, that the storm would spend itself in its allotted time, and go its way? Hiram and his family in their house beyond the cocal, were they safe? And Richard's house, empty and lonely in the gale . . . It seemed to me that an empty house must be more vulnerable than those with people inside, even frightened people . . . Richard, Richard, where are you?

Zoé stood at the window. She seemed electrified.

"Look! Look, Olive!"

She had opened a shutter, and beyond it was a rift in the batten blind. By a flash of lightning I saw waves rising monstrously. The air was filled with rain and sheets of spray. I glimpsed the light on Beacon Key.

The windows began to press inward. I drew back as a barrage of shells and pebbles battered the blinds. Zoé had already drawn away, was swaying and pirouetting in grave ecstasy. All the candle flames were veering one way. The flame of the lamp veered too, blackening the chimney. Zoé's shells rattled in their cabinet.

How could any house resist so powerful a will to destroy it? Yonder Key seemed small, a crumb in the path of the devouring ocean. Surely if the sea desired it could swallow it . . . Richard, in your little boat, are you all right?

I walked the floor, murmuring snatches of familiar words. *"The Lord on high is mightier than the noise of many waters, yea, than the mighty waves of the sea."* . . . *"He holdeth the wind in his fists."* . . . *"Now I lay me down to sleep . . ."*

"Where is the chapel, Zoé?"

She paused in her dancing, gazed at me.

"There's a chapel," I said. "Show me where it is. A chapel."

She nodded. "If you will let me carry the candle."

I said nothing, and she took the tallest one. I blew out the others and followed her, carrying the lamp with its hurricane shade and a box of matches. We went down the hall, Zoé's thin green dress blowing in some unaccountable draft, the carpet rippling beneath our feet, the rain hammering on the roof, nailing it down, so that the murderous, bellowing, raging wind wouldn't tear it off.

"Listen!" Zoé stopped, clutching my arm. "Ghosts," she said. "Listen."

I did hear it, even in the unspeakable din—sounds that were no part of the storm, hoarse singing and great gusts of laughter, a ringing as of tankards on a wooden table, thunderous yet hollow, mere shells of sound.

Zoé pointed with her candle at a door swinging open on a vast blackness, clanging shut, swinging open in that strange draft. The singing, the laughter and ringing were the same, whether the door was open or shut . . . A wassail. I remembered Nannine's words. Old Jared Croome and his cronies, Richard had said . . . The old banquet hall.

The door clanged shut and Zoé flew past it like an escaping bird, turned a corner into another passage. When I reached that corner she had disappeared. There was no sign of a door, no sign that the passage led anywhere at all.

Suddenly, just ahead, the wall opened, and Zoé, holding up her candle, looked out at me. She seemed impatient, as if she were still flying from the wassail ghosts. Quickly she drew me into her niche and slid the panel shut. We went up a spiral stair, entered a corridor, black-dark except for our lights, and so silent that we could hear our feet on the stone floor. One might hide in this windowless place and not know there was a storm outside.

Why should a chapel be buried so deep?

The corridor ended in a door, black as teakwood, and intricately carved. It opened to us, and here was the storm again, flashing outside the stained windows, lighting up a long room, roaring and lashing against its walls. There were no pews or chairs.

Zoé moved to a central shrine, held her candle to the candles there till one by one the flames stole out of the darkness, shining before what appeared to be a statue of the Virgin. Its attitude was pensive and full of grace. The long robe of alabaster or white jade flowed smoothly to its feet. Around the neck someone had hung a necklace of blue stones.

"Kwan-Yin," said Zoé, touching the slender hands.

I set my lamp on a nearby stand, almost displacing the grinning effigy that sat there. I looked at it, and looked away, saw others, fierce or sinister or obscene, an army of idols all around us. They stirred and shook, rocked by the storm, seeming to chuckle, to ogle, to mock and threaten, to stare with horrible eyes. Only Kwan-Yin remained composed, gazing down at her candles.

The old Croomes brought back things, Nannine had said.

I blew the candles out, but Zoé delayed, standing in a sort of trance till a drop of hot wax falling on her hand startled her, and she held her candle straight and followed me.

The door opened before we reached it. There was the light

of an electric torch, the figure of a man. Ezra's voice spoke to me.

"Miss Johanna wishes to see you."

Miss Johanna wished to see me. In the dead of night, with the hurricane howling, Miss Johanna commanded me to come. What if I refused?

Ezra stood aside that Zoé and I might pass through the door and down the corridor. I was not certain that he followed, but scorned to look behind. I led the way down the spiral stair, past the ghostly carousal . . .

Who would stay with Zoé if I went down to Miss Johanna?

Nannine was waiting in the tower.

"Better go," she said, taking my lamp. Her hand shook. She was mortally afraid of storms.

Better go. Why did we both obey the nod of that woman enthroned in the inner darkness of this house like a black and deadly spider in the center of its web? What had the storm roused in her that she demanded to see me after nothing but silence?

A hideous scream of the wind and the crash of some object against the walls sent stronger vibrations through the tower. There came a louder groaning and beating of the rain.

Zoé, with no other music, began again her eerie dance.

Nannine's white and pleading face came close to mine. She thrust a candle into my hand.

"Go, or she'll blame me. Here, take your matches. The lights are off."

I had thought the storm must be worse in the upper regions of the house. It seemed, however, more violent as I descended, as if the wind were sucking at the lower walls, tearing at their roots. The miasma I had always felt was heavier now, moving in black, drowning waves, as if its dregs were stirred. I pushed through it with my flickering, fainting candle.

Miss Johanna's door stood open.

"Come in," she said in a voice as hollow as the ghost voices upstairs.

She sat in her wheel chair as she had sat the night I came. A kerosene lamp was on the table beside her, a glass and a bottle of Scotch whisky.

I had not known Miss Johanna drank, had supposed her the soul of sobriety. Perhaps she had wished to dull her sensibilities at this frightening time. "Sit down," she said, offering me none of her anodyne.

I put my candle on the table and sat before her as I had sat that other night. She looked different now. The graying hair that had been smoothly done was uncombed and disheveled, the housecoat she wore damply spotted as if some of the whisky had been spilled. She looked older, unkempt, her hands gripping the arms of her chair, her black eyes burning in their sockets.

I thought, The center of the web.

The wind was quieter here, though still a battering, raging fact. Perhaps it only seemed less in the presence of Miss Johanna.

She spoke, still in that hollow voice.

"I have sent for you because I want to talk with you. I have put it off too long, giving you your head, watching to see how far you'd go. Do you hear? Do you understand?"

"Yes. I understand."

I met her burning eyes, hating my voice for its faintness.

Was I afraid? I could rise and go out that door, and she could not follow. Yet I had no will, no wish to go. Numbness had come over me, lethargy. I thought of the soldier in India, and said to myself, "Two and two are four."

"I suppose you know," said Miss Johanna, "that I do not like you. Not that you have defied me openly. Nothing so honest. What you did was ingratiate yourself with that old man, my father. I'd like to know your motive. Did you think he would alter his will in your favor? Answer me. Was that your aim?"

"No. That's ridiculous."

"Ridiculous, indeed. He had no notion of altering his will, and he will never do it. However, you cajoled him into supporting your whims with Zoé, persuaded him to let you indulge her, cater to her, increase her mania, even to stop her visits with me; wormed out of him a commercial secret, our propagation of the wax palm, the carnauba from British Guiana. What do you hope to gain by that?"

"Nothing. It was—"

"Do you deny that you pried about the attic, went into trunks and boxes, hunting out this family's personal affairs? Do you deny it?"

"Yes, yes. That was never my—"

She leaned toward me, lowering her voice.

"I have known when you took Zoé to the bay side and to Richard Lowrie's house. I have known when you went to that house alone. What you do on your afternoons off is your own affair, but what you have done to my sister is not. And your entering my attic in the dead of night, opening trunks of private papers . . . How many people would not have had you arrested?"

"I was looking for Zoé's clothes."

"So you said. And you went later into Muspa and had so-called duplicates made of them. With my father's permission, of course. It's easy enough to cajole an old, sick man. You got Zoé dressed in those clothes, rousing her subconscious in every way you could. What have you ferreted out? What do you know? Answer me."

Her incandescent eyes gazed fixedly into mine.

I thought of Zoé's diary. Its pages were photographed before my eyes. I thought of Zoé's watch.

I roused myself. Blessed are the— Blessed are the—what? Two-times-two is four.

"I know nothing," I said. "And I had no motive except to make Zoé happy. Judge Croome wants the same thing. That's why he helped me."

"To make Zoé happy," she repeated, settling back in her chair. "And suppose she is happy for a little while. Such indulgences can lead only to her remembering. Then we'll have a violent maniac on our hands. I warned you the night you came, but you did as you pleased."

"I spoke to Judge Croome. My correspondence had been with him."

"I see. You spoke to him, instead of to me, because you knew that what you were doing was wrong, and you used undue influence to bring him around. He had always pampered Zoé, but his pampering hadn't been a senseless digging up of her memories. You told me that you had had no experience with the psychotic, no training, yet you have used skillfully a system that we have avoided. And this Zoé—this Zoé whom you coddle and pet, is a viper. That was why she went insane. Her own sins came back on her. Man thinks he can avoid the consequences of his evil act. He is a fool. His crime completes its inevitable circle to return and crush him."

There was a fusillade as of coconuts and small debris against the blinds.

The voice went on.

"That imbecile upstairs is a thief. You were in the attic. You opened my box. You saw the satin cloth, the veil, the gloves and shoes. You supposed they were hers, but they were not. They were mine. He loved me—*me*." She beat her breast, lowering her voice, staring at me still. "A snake, a thief, coming home with her baby ways, so gay and innocent. I have to laugh! And he, the fool, like all men where a new face is concerned, if a woman is determined— Yes, she was able to do it.

"But she brought him death. He died by her hand as surely as if she had held the rifle that killed him. If it had not been for her, he would not have been there, hunting in the grove, tripping over a root, shooting himself. She was with him. They found her sitting with his head in her lap, his blood on her dress, a gibbering maniac."

I thought, That last night—in the grove. Hunting at midnight. An accident . . .

"A mad woman," said Miss Johanna, "all that year. A year she does not remember, whatever she may remember of what went before or of what happened yesterday. Nine long months when she turned from a slim girl into a shapeless disgrace, swelling, festering, with his child.

"I could walk then. I could climb stairs. But they guarded

179

her, Belen and my father. They kept me out of her room the night the child was born. Dr. Lowrie said I was too distraught, too anxious. They kept me out, but I heard her screams. I listened. I stood outside her door and heard nature's revenge for their ecstasy. I forbade chloroform, forbade them to give it to her. I said that another doctor had told us that she had a heart like our mother's, one of those hearts that, though perfectly normal in other respects, succumbs under chloroform or ether. They were afraid to risk it—my father, Belen, Dr. Lowrie. They were afraid.

"Screaming, screaming my beloved's name, tasting to the full every pang, every burning agony. All that night, all the next day, till the child was born.

"What do you think now of your pure, your beautiful Zoé? Perhaps you are no better than she is, only smarter. Your generation is smart. You outwit nature, but you flinch as we did at illegitimacy. You hide it as we did, feel its disgrace. Smart, yet totally without logic.

"They think I don't know what they did with the child, all those thirty years ago. Schuyler Winn's child. They wouldn't tell me, but I know. I've always known who he is. They fixed it up between them, my father and Dr. Lowrie. They slipped the baby out, and never told me till it was gone.

"Why should they think I would harm the child? *She* was to blame, and Skee was dead. I would never harm Skee's child.

"And now you appear and try to dig it all up. I haven't stopped you because my father has been on your side. He used to see things my way, now it's your way. You want to make Zoé remember that hour in the grove, to see Skee's face on her lap and her own hands wet with his blood; to cling to him again when they took him away from her, laughing and screaming and tearing her hair. Yes, they do that. Tearing out her own hair, trying to drown herself.

"Let me tell you this. My father can't champion you now. He's helpless, can hardly speak. I could put you out—now, tonight. I could call Ezra and have him put you out in the hurricane, let you be torn to bits, blown into the bay, beaten to death. It would serve you right, for it isn't as if you hadn't had your warning—the very night you came.

"Well, you may not know it, but I have a deep regard for my father. If he asked for you—which he has not—I'd want to produce you. It's no more than that. But don't try me too far. I am mistress here. Remember that.

"And now get out," sitting tall in her chair, her eyes blazing under her tousled hair, her voice low and threatening. "Get out of this room."

I wonder now why I did not reply to Miss Johanna, whether instinct told me that any retort would be folly, or whether I was too frightened by her mention of Ezra and the storm. With her last words I felt a sense of physical release, as if some string by which she had been holding me had been cut. I picked up my candle in silence and went out, fighting my way through the mists of the hall and stairs, back to the tower.

Nannine looked at me questioningly, curious even amid the storm as to what Miss Johanna had wanted. I gave her back her candle, and she went out. We had neither said a word.

Zoé was in bed, sleeping through the hurricane. One arm

flung above her shining head, the lashes dark on her cheek, her young lips parted with her quiet breath.

I stood looking down at her.

Somewhere she had a child as old as I—older.

No, she must not remember. She must never remember.

Stirring, she opened her eyes.

"Olive!" she cried, and caught my hand. "I dreamed you had gone away. I dreamed Papa died, and you went away."

I dreamed. She knew the dream from the reality. She knew the dream for the first time since I had come to Yonder.

Holding my hand, she laid her cheek against it.

"I'm glad you're here. I'm glad you're not gone."

She knew the dream.

XIX

Richard came back two weeks later. Came back with no preliminary cable or letter, having made harbor in Port au Prince before the hurricane. He had contrived to get all reports regarding Florida and our island, but had not bothered to send out reports concerning himself.

"No wonder Marcia left you."

"Oh, I always cabled Marcia. I cabled my mother, too."

"Anybody who cared," I suggested. "Well, there were people on Yonder who cared and worried, too. Nannine told me that Judge Croome kept saying your name during the hurricane. He remembered where you were. Zoé remembered, too. So did I."

"I'll do better next time."

He had brought us presents. For Zoé a bracelet of small pink cameos, bought in Port au Prince; for me a ring hammered from an old coin and set with a smoky pearl he had found in a conch off a spice island near Damballa Oueddo.

Nannine sat with Zoé while he took me to our favorite hang-out, the Barnacle. The Barnacle stirred me to confidences, as it had before. I told him about my interview with Miss Johanna, though I had resolved not to mention it. Why I shrank from revealing to him the mystery about Zoé I don't know. Perhaps to tell seemed like a betrayal of her. Yet I told him, watching its effect while he sat looking out over the bay, quiet tonight under a star-strewn sky.

"So that was it," he said, and I knew that he had never heard the tale before.

"But hunting," I reminded him. "Hunting at midnight. Is that plausible?"

"Oh, yes. Raccoons."

"Do they hunt raccoons with guns?"

"I suppose they could."

"Zoé's lover was not hunting," I said. And I told him about Zoé's diary, and how it dovetailed in its way with Miss Johanna's account, up to that last breathless meeting when they planned to elope next morning. "After they said good-night Zoé heard voices, and ran back. That was all. That was when time stopped for Zoé, but Miss Johanna's account goes on. . . . Strange your father didn't tell you what happened."

"No." Richard's gaze came back to me. "He wouldn't have done that. And I wasn't interested."

But now he was interested. A sort of heaviness had come over him.

"And she knows where the child is," he said. "Miss Johanna, I mean."

"So she claims."

"It's probably true. I'm sure all she told you is true."

He believed her. Perhaps his father had believed her, too. Perhaps everyone had always believed her.

We were both silent after that. Some of Richard's heaviness had been communicated to me. Yet I had needed to tell him. It was too much to bear alone.

But the telling had not helped me.

I thought of Dane's words: I never made a confidence I didn't regret.

I had written to Dane shortly after Leonie's death, the usual letter of condolence, painful and difficult to write. To my surprise, he replied, though he might have invoked the exemption accorded to those in grief.

"You were always kind," he wrote. "Always understanding. I am sorry Leonie did not know you well. You would have liked each other . . . It is a strange thing to miss someone. I knew the sensation for the first time when you went away. To pass the house you had lived in, to see the new rector's children playing on the lawn the way you and Pony used to play, disturbed me at first. I guess I'm set in my ways. . . . Leonie. It never occurred to me that she would leave me. I think none of us thought of that." He broke off, as if he could not linger with his tragedy. "Mother says you are happy," he wrote. "You deserve happiness. Thank you for your sympathy, Olive. As always, Dane."

I kept this letter which, strangely enough, was the only one I had ever received from Dane. I might have answered it, might have developed a correspondence there. I told myself that I had little time and less to write about. Dane was not interested in the activities of Yonder, in my care of Zoé, and my sinister war with Miss Johanna, in the illness of Judge Croome, my visits with Richard.

Few visits with Richard now, buried as he was in the first draft of a new book, though Zoé, forgetting he had returned, gathered flowers now and then, and took them to his house, surprised when she heard him inside, typing away. On these occasions she would lay the flowers at his door, and join me where I waited among the trees.

One day on my afternoon off he invited me to his house for coffee. I found Marcia there, Marcia and her twin boys. She was a pretty girl, this person to whom Richard had once been married, inclined to plumpness, with brown bobbed hair curling from one of the tight cloches we wore in those days, and gray, rather pensive eyes, behind dark-rimmed glasses. In Richard's house she appeared to take charge, pouring the coffee, and asking Floyd to bring some seagrape jelly.

"They expect it," she explained to me, indicating the boys who sat together on the divan, four years old, and as alike as two robins. She asked Richard about his new island, and he was sketchy in his replies. She would have to read his book, he said, and she,

"Don't forget to send it."

This was a farewell call, Luke, her husband, having taken a position in a northern laboratory. She and the boys were joining him that week. They had sold the old Lowrie home that she had lived in with Richard, and that had fallen to her when they separated.

"I hope you'll go on with Richard's typing," she said to

me. I promised that I would, if he would let me, as long as I was on Yonder.

"Oh, he'll let you. He says you're good. I'm jealous," she added, laughing. "I thought I was the only one who could type to suit him."

The boys were restless, having finished the jelly. Wandering about, they explored the room, and presently we were conversing to the accompaniment of the tom-tom.

"Boys!" cried Marcia, then despairing of making them hear, she added, "They saw Fo-Fum today. I seldom go to see him—it upsets him. But I thought I ought to say good-by."

Fo-Fum. Mrs. Frisbie's boxer. The captain coming home, a stranger . . .

"How's he looking?" asked Richard.

"Oh, fine. It was odd, but he took to the boys. She keeps him on the side porch. Seems fond of him."

Marcia said she must go now, there was so much to do.

Richard invited me to cross the bay with them, but I felt they should have that last ride alone.

I could hear the sound of the tom-tom as I went down the beach road.

"No," said Richard when I asked him, "Fo-Fum was not to blame. Merely one of the straws in the wind, straws that tell us no woman should marry an explorer."

"She could have gone with you," I said.

"No. Marcia hates the sea."

"How could you marry a woman who hates the sea?"

"Now you've gone back to the beginning. All mistakes could be avoided if we stopped before they began. And then there was Luke."

"Yes, Luke. When did he come in?"

"He was already there. Marcia had wanted to spend a winter in Florida, so she got herself a job here. She was that kind of girl. In no time at all, she had a choice of two husbands. Marrying an explorer seemed to her less dull than marrying a man who worked indoors with wires and gadgets. She learned better, of course. I told her finally I'd give up the sea. She was as skeptical of the promise as if it had been made by a whale. All the same, I tried to keep it, and I think my restlessness— Well, it must have been pretty awful, poor kid. What could I do but set her free? She and Luke have had something of a struggle, but he's landed now."

He seemed to be relieved. Seemed to have something off his mind.

XX

Zoé and I were at breakfast one morning when Ezra brought
me a telegram. Usually Nannine gave me what mail I received. From Ezra's hand the message seemed ominous.

"This has been opened," I said, observing how crudely the
flap had been separated and sealed again.

"A mistake," he answered.

I closed the door.

The wire was from Dane.

"En route to Miami. Stopping off on Yonder this afternoon."

Pain caught at my heart. Happiness. Shock. Dane on
Yonder. This afternoon. Dane—here.

"Let me see it," whispered Zoé, and taking it in her hand,
"Who is Dane?"

"Your cousin," I answered.

"My cousin. Dane. Nelly Dane. Nelly. Helen Dane Carrington . . . But we're going to Richard's," she added.

Yes, we had promised to have lunch with Richard.

After our vigil on the beach I went to Richard's house, told
him that company was coming.

"Dane?" he asked.

"Dane," I answered, wondering how he had guessed.

He said, "I'll get word to Belen. We'll have our meeting tomorrow. How about Zoé? Who's staying with her?"

I told him I had exchanged afternoons with Nannine.

He offered me the loan of his car to meet the ferry, but Dane, as it turned out, arrived by hired launch on his own schedule.

I was not told when he came. Ezra admitted him, showed him at once to the parlors where Miss Johanna (accustomed, no doubt, to guests landing from their own or borrowed boats) sat in her special hostess chair awaiting him. At his insistence, I learned later, she finally rang for Nannine and dispatched her to find me just as I was leaving for the ferry.

"That woman!" he said to me, when we were liberated and making for the launch. "How do you put up with her?"

In the parlors he had been obliged to put up with her himself. When I went in he had greeted me with obvious relief and made immediate sounds of departure.

"You can't go now," Miss Johanna informed him. "I've ordered tea."

If anyone had told me that Dane would sit down at that, reluctant, it is true, but obedient, I would not have believed it. He sat, however, and I sat, too, while we looked at each other. It seemed to me that he had grown older in these months, thinner, too, yet still the radiant Dane, impeccably dressed, his blond hair ruffled by the bay wind.

I heard the creak of the tea wagon as Ezra came down the hall, saw for the first time the ornate gold tea service, the exquisite Nankin cups, smelled the aroma of China tea.

There were plates of piping hot muffins, of crusty little cakes, dark with nuts and raisins, and enough seagrape jelly to have satisfied Marcia's boys.

Miss Johanna poured from the golden urn, her ringed hands unaffected by her illness. She had intended to ignore me, but Dane brought me his own cup, accepted another, answering meanwhile the questions that my appearance had interrupted. Those questions having arrived at Pony, Miss Johanna learned of her remarriage the week before. As she had never been told of Pony's widowhood, grass or sod, Dane was obliged to go back a little, while she took notice of me and my negligence with a malevolent glance. She looked handsome, dressed in violet crepe with sapphire brooch and earrings.

Tea over, she said that Dane must play for her, then he might go.

And there he was, sitting down at the piano, playing *The Dance of the Night Herons*, glancing at me, himself, and smiling; playing bits from his ballet, while I saw in my mind the parsonage living room, and the fire burning in the grate . . . How different the ballet was on this piano, with its fluent, singing tone. This was the Chickering upright that had been Miss Johanna's as a girl, that she sometimes played even now. In the dead of night, Nannine said, she would demand to be taken to it, unable to sleep till she had played and played like something mad. Leschetizky, Chopin, Bach, Grieg—flying echoes through the dark house.

Dane rose, and Miss Johanna said, "Father and I expect you back for dinner."

Dane demurred, doubted if he could manage it.

"We will wait till you come," Miss Johanna said firmly, and Dane answered, "Oh, well . . . thank you. Fine."

"Seven o'clock," said Miss Johanna.

At last we got away.

Richard was down at the boathouse, curious, I knew, to meet Dane. They stood a while talking together, talking about boats, about fishing, so that it was late when we finally boarded the hired launch, urged by Dane's wish to escape from Yonder.

"Who's this Lowrie?" he asked.

"The explorer," I said. "Explorer and writer. He lives on Yonder. Some people find it fascinating."

"So I gather."

"Tell me about Pony," with the spray dashing in our faces. "Did she marry well?"

"I don't know. *He* did."

"I hope she's happy this time."

"Well, the guy's a lot older than she is. Maybe that's good."

"And Dorilys. How do you pronounce it?"

"That's right. Dorilee. She's getting to look like something. Up to now she's been hardly more than a lump."

We puttered past the Barnacle, and Dane, who had partaken sparingly of Miss Johanna's tea, suggested that we go ashore for dinner. For some reason, I didn't want to go to the Barnacle with Dane. I reminded him of his promise to Miss Johanna. I could imagine the banquet she had planned in his honor, intending that reports of surviving splendor should go back to the Carringtons.

Dane, however, released from the spell of Miss Johanna's

presence, made light of his promise, and later, when the water had been dark for some time, we stopped at the pier of a beach hotel, a Moorish palace, whose towers and white façade I had often seen from the bay side.

There was only a sprinkling of guests in the dining room. From our nook among the ferns I became conscious of the music, the subdued lights and dimly shining tables. Yes, this was the proper setting for a dinner with Dane. But I would certainly hear of that flouted promise to Miss Johanna.

"You look wonderful in red, Olive."

Dane's voice across the bowl of white frangipani flowers.

I told him that the dress was a suppressed desire. "A suppressed desire, coming up for air."

"Why suppressed, since it suits you?"

"Does it? I've always heard that blue suited me—cool, misty blue."

"I know better," said Dane's low voice.

I felt a flush move up my face, was glad when the waiter returned with our cocktails.

"Tell me about Leonie," I said, not meaning to be tactless, or to evoke any ghost, only to dispel the ghost he had just raised.

He looked down into his glass.

"We were not happy," he answered.

"I'm sorry," I said, confused.

"She wasn't well," he added. "The baby business started almost at once. Leonie was spoiled, poor kid—spoiled and neglected. I know you're thinking I was spoiled, too, but I wasn't. Pony was the pet. Fritz and I—

"Oh, well. Then there was the house. Leonie wanted the

house. She had a decorator, of course, but decisions, people waiting for her decisions—that was all hard on her. Her parents were in Europe, and they wouldn't have been much help anyhow, for they didn't want us to live to ourselves. Leonie was building the house while they were away. She really needed her mother's help, somebody's help."

"Couldn't your mother—"

"Yes, if she'd known. If any of us had realized. She used to appeal to me—Leonie, I mean. Should she let the decorator paint peacocks on the nursery wall? He said it was the newest thing, but did it seem like a baby? Would rabbits be better? I said it didn't matter, the baby wouldn't notice. It wasn't that I had no interest, though she used to cry and say that was it. I can't bear to see those rabbits now, the only decision I ever knew her to make. I wonder if you can understand, I mean my not helping her more."

"Yes. Most men are like that."

"I just wanted her to have what she wanted, and she didn't always know what that was."

"It's a pity," I said, "that you had only those first months. It might have been different afterward."

"It might. She was a nice kid."

I asked, leaving the dark waters of Leonie, "Do you suppose Pony will ever come home?"

"Oh, yes. I think so. She and her baron will come wagging in some day."

"A baron?"

"She's the Baroness d'Aguesseau-Rouziers. Are you impressed?"

I remember every moment of that evening with Dane. I

think not a word he spoke is forgotten, nor a movement of his hands, nor the look on his face. I remember the scent of the frangipani in the bowl between us, and how he drew one of the flowers through his buttonhole, so that I smelled it closer when we danced. I remember the exotic flavor of the lobster Bombay—curried, with cheese and shredded coconut —the strawberries, the *café diabolique,* brought flaming to our table.

Dancing, we kept to our sequestered corner among the ferns. I thought, Am I actually with Dane? Why am I not so happy as before he came, as when I knew he was on the way? The prospect of his coming had been more disturbing than his arrival, more potent than his arm around me now. Is it that our minds soar to rarer heights when unhampered by the body, that the body is cumbersome to take along, gets in the way? Not always. But there was not the bliss in this event that I had anticipated, nor even that I had known in those dream journeys I took with him when I was twelve . . . Still, he was Dane, the long-desired, the unattainable. Dane, free. Dane, *here.*

He said while we were dancing, "I'm taking you back with me, Olive."

"How?" I laughed.

"You'll see. I'll manage."

And as we lingered over the coffee, "Do you remember the last time we were together?"

"Of course," I said.

"It makes you angry to think of it. If you knew how often I've thought of it, myself. The suddenness of it, of finding that I loved you, the—the feeling that you loved me, too. How could that happen? How could a thing like that be buried in a man and he not know?"

"It couldn't."

"It was, and I think you knew."

"I certainly didn't know about you."

"Women always know. Did you know about yourself? That is, if you really— If I guessed right, that is."

"Yes, I knew about that."

"You might have told me," reproachfully. "I'd have told *you* if I'd known."

We laughed a little, Dane crushing out his cigarette.

"Why didn't you tell me, Olive—at once?"

"You would have laughed, Dane. Almost anyone would have laughed. I didn't know it was something one told. And the older I got, the harder it would have been."

"Yet you told me that last night, not in words. You told me when it was too late. It's harder to break an engagement at that point than it is to get a divorce. Believe me, I tried. I asked Leonie— No matter. I love you, Olive. I want you to go back with me. I want you to marry me as soon as—as soon as you will."

Why did I not say that I would go back with him, marry him at any time?

He said, "Don't answer me now. You think it's too soon after Leonie's death to talk about these things."

"No, Dane. Not that."

"It may be too soon, of course. But there were times when I thought I must speak to you, even when Leonie was alive. What would you have done if I had?"

"I don't know. I'm glad you didn't come then."

"Perhaps I wouldn't have come—unless you had told me to. But if I could have phoned you . . . I forgot, if I ever knew, that there was no phone on Yonder. I picked up the receiver late one night when you'd been gone about a month. I felt I must hear your voice. I asked for Yonder. They said they could reach the key by telegram, that was all. You were really gone—out of hearing."

The dead of night. How strange it would have been. Ezra coming up the stairs. A knock on my door. "The telephone, Miss York." The lighting of the candle. The descent of the stairs, wondering . . . Dane's voice . . .

"Would you have told me to come?" he asked now. "Would you have let me?"

I said, "Probably. I was capable of anything."

"It's different now, I gather. You've changed," he said.

He smoked in silence, then he smiled.

"I had a French teacher once who quoted Hamlet. He said, 'Ficklety, thy name is woman.' He was so right. I thought you were something apart, a fixed star. You were serious, even as a child. Mystifying. I used to wonder about you."

"Was that why you told me to be light and brittle?"

"God, what patter!"

"You see, you didn't tell me the truth any more than I told you."

"I didn't know the truth—not then. And now you've changed."

"I wanted to change," I said. "That's what I came here to do, if I could. I came, meaning to forget you. I couldn't at first because you followed me. Not really, but you were still on the beach, a little boy playing with his pail and shovel in

197

the sand. I was always seeing you—when I went out, when I stood at the window in my room, there you were—a little boy in yellow trunks—you, *you*."

"I remember those trunks," he said a bit dreamily.

I stared at him. "You mean they really were—yellow?"

"Always. Uncle used to call me The Yellow Kid, after some comic strip character of his day. I liked yellow."

"But you never told me. I never saw you wear that color in my life. I just— No one told me."

He stared back at me. "That's odd. Did I finally go away?"

"I don't know. After I heard Leonie was going to have a child I didn't see you any more."

He said, "That place does things to people. If you'd marry me and come home with me, or even just come home, you'd be yourself again. I'd have a chance of winning you back to yourself."

"It's not Yonder," I said after a pause. "It's me. I don't think I'm fickle. I think something died inside me. I'm sorry, Dane."

He smiled. "Don't mention it," he said, mocking his own best manner, putting away his cigarette case. "Don't think about it a minute."

The night was cloudy as we went home, a smell of rain was in the air. We were silent against the spray, the putter of the motor. I did not try to talk, to salvage our evening. It was too terrible a thing that I had refused to marry Dane. Unthinkable. He had made no attempt to take up with me where he had left off, but had asked me to be his wife. I had not even opened my hand to receive this golden fruit. Was I avenging the humiliation of his long indifference? No, for I bore him no ill-will, had enjoyed loving him for the most part. Perhaps indeed it was Yonder that had done this to us. Perhaps the feeling which seemed to have died might be stirred into life again if I went back with him. Tomorrow, no doubt, I would wonder that I let him go home alone. It would be too late then. If I knew Dane, he would never ask me again.

The boat scraped the pier, and he helped me out. I suggested that we take the beach road which was longer, but not so dark. He refused, saying that he had to get back to his train. We entered the shadows of the red mangroves and buttonwood trees, followed the white path into the grove. The dank swamp smell rushed out at us, and a wave of small, flapping, startled things—bats, perhaps. I thought of snakes, hating Dane for his stubbornness, then, stumbling, fell against him. He caught and held me in the utter blackness. "Olive —Olive!" The voice I had heard that day in the study. His arms were tight, his mouth closed over mine. I seemed to die of that kiss, yet the instant it was over I felt my hands pushing him away, found myself running blindly, in terror of the place, of the dark, of the kiss itself, for they all seemed one.

A light shone through the trees, and I knew that it was Richard's, knew that I had left the path that was a short cut through the grove. If I kept on to the left a bit, I would come out on the beach road as I had come that day with Richard, facing Pirate's Finger. I would be safely out of the grove, but Dane—Dane could not possibly know the place except by the two trips he had made through it today. Perhaps he would go back to the boat, for how could he see to follow me?

I was ashamed of my fear, and, though still sick with it, turned back, walking as carefully as I could and calling to him. Once I thought he answered, then suddenly he was close to me. I grasped his arm.

"I'm afraid of this place," I said.

He answered, "We should have a torch," and got out his cigarette lighter, snapped on its trivial flame. The grove did not disturb him any more than it did Richard.

"I could have guided us through," I told him. "I can still do it, though we've left the path. That light through the trees. If we just keep to the left here, straight ahead—"

I held to his arm and we went on, walking carefully behind his light. We came out on the beach road. A drop of rain fell on my hand.

"You didn't need to run from me, Olive."

"Not from you," I answered. "There's death in the grove. Zoé's lover was killed there. That's what drove her insane."

"I see. If I'd known how you felt—"

"I understand. It's over now."

We walked on in silence till he said,

"How can you part with me like this?"

"Don't go tonight," I answered. "Stay a little while."

"Will it be different tomorrow?"

"Perhaps. Oh, Dane, why must it be this way? Why couldn't you have loved me all the years that I loved you?"

"I think I did. The parsonage was—well, not the atmosphere for a pagan like me. Not till that last evening, when I found out what you were."

"What was I? A potential—?"

"Don't say it. I adore your potentials."

We came to the house, mounted the steps of the porte-cochère. He drew me against him, kissed me again.

"Goodnight, Olive. Good-by."

We stood there in silence with his arms around me.

"Give me your key," he said.

He opened the door, went inside with me.

Richard came into the hall from the direction of Judge Croome's room. He asked about our evening, took it for granted that Dane was spending the night.

Dane did not linger in the house. He went out with Richard, and I was glad. He would have a torch and company going through the grove.

Or perhaps they would take the beach road.

XXI

I was helping Judge Croome, helping him to walk. He leaned on my shoulder, dragging his feet. It was a dream, and like Zoé's dream it led down a dark road. Only I was not flying, but trudging, helping the old man, helping him to escape from the strong pursuing wind. Eyes like lights stared up from the ground, and the cloudy sky dropped closer, became fog pressing around us, black, suffocating . . .

If only the old man could walk faster . . .

I must have moaned or cried out, for Zoé was beside me. "Poor Olive!"

A small wraith, hovering dimly. Rain was coming into the room. I rose and closed all the windows. She was in my bed when I came back. Her arms went round me as I got in. She began to croon, patting my arm.

> "Moon it am a-shinin' in the heaven up above.
> Turtle am a-pinin' for his little lady love . . .
> Close your eyes an' sleep. . . ."

Nannine had said when I came upstairs that Miss Johanna had waited dinner for us. She had worn the black lace dress and her diamonds, had directed the preparation of dinner—and such a dinner! Mr. Lowrie had been invited. Finally, they sat down, just the two of them. She was furious.

"I suppose she blamed me," I said.

"Well, she didn't say so. Afterward they sat in Judge Croome's room, and Mr. Lowrie read some of his new book to them. I guess he thinks the judge won't live to see it in print. It entertained the old man a lot. He almost forgot about not seeing Mr. Carrington, though he was mighty disappointed at first. He'd been looking forward to it."

I felt angry with Dane. A visit with him would have done his uncle good. How could he have been so heartless, for surely he had known the old man was ill. Now it was too late. They would never meet again.

Nor would Dane and I. Somehow I had known all along that I was not through with Dane, that I would see him again. Yet I had supposed our meeting would be merely a new design in the old web of frustration, frustration that was oddly less disturbing than the confusion I felt now. I told myself again, before I fell asleep, that tomorrow I would be sorry I had let him go.

Now as I lay beside Zoé I thought, This is tomorrow. This is tomorrow, and I am not sorry. Once the love of Dane had been the whole of me, my identity, my history. It could die only if I died myself. I had died. I had died, and lived still, renewed, reborn. It occurred to me that we should not fear death, for we experience it many times, and resurrection, too, before we're through.

I went back to sleep while the rain stopped, and the gray light moved off the sea into the room. Zoé was gone when I woke, was in her room, nude as Aphrodite, brushing her hair before the mirror.

"This is the day," she said softly.

"And a fine one," I answered, as I so often did.

"This is the day," sitting with the brush lax in her hand, gazing out into the light.

I was never to hear her say it again.

Life is too full of melodrama. The artist, recording it, corrects its balder outlines, mutes or heightens its colors, avoids the coincidences of which it is made, the cliché, the commonplace.

I have no skill in such matters, a middle-aged wife and mother who, in 1930–31, saw these things happen, and now, twenty-five years later, wonders if the part she played in them was good or evil. Life had prepared me for the experience on Yonder, had hammered and shaped me, and placed me there. So the thing I blindly brought to pass must have been right. And yet I don't know.

Bear with me. I can only tell it as it was.

Zoé wore the white mull dress for the last time, the blue sash. Nannine had washed and ironed the dress, and though it would never be the same, it was still beautiful. The sash was new, and the small blue locket I had given her at Christmas.

I never saw her happier than when we went out that morning, parting at the cabaña which had been found inland after the hurricane and restored. The beach chairs had been locked inside it, and though battered, were in their old places, side by side.

I watched Zoé move with a gull-like motion, following the curve of beach to the jetty. There she stood, a slim white figure, her skirts, her bright hair, blowing back, as she had stood that day on the bay-side reef . . . Nothing, nothing in sight, not even a fishing boat. Only the vast blue ocean, the vaster blue sky.

She sat down in the shade of the palm trees to watch and to wait. I opened the book I had brought and began to read.

"Good morning."

Dane's voice over my shoulder.

My heart turned over, like an old dog who has not forgotten painfully learned tricks.

"Feeling better?" he asked.

I looked up at him, standing in front of me now, immaculate, radiant, as if he had slept well, breakfasted well.

I replaced the marker, closed the book.

"I thought you'd gone," I said.

He sat down beside me. "Thanks for not saying you *hoped* I'd gone." Smiling, challenging me to protest.

"I'm glad you didn't go. I asked you last night to stay."

"I know. And I couldn't leave after scaring you like that, making you run."

I would not explain again that it was the grove. He would never understand.

"All right now?" he asked.

I said, "I'm never afraid in the daytime. How did you come —by launch again?"

"I never left. It was raining and your friend, Lowrie, took me in. Comfortable room, comfortable bed, and Olive just next door. Where's your charge?"

I indicated Zoé under the palm trees.

He watched her a moment, frowning against the sun.

"I seem to remember her doing that. Watching for her boy friend, isn't that it?"

"He was killed," I said, "the night before they were to be married."

"I remember. Hunting. Fell, and his gun went off. And she goes on watching. I suppose a woman has to go crazy to be as faithful as that. It must grow monotonous."

"No, because she forgets from day to day."

His gaze came back to me.

"I don't mean Zoé. I was thinking of you—a girl like you—marooned in a job like this. You say you're not bored."

"I'm not. I love your cousin. I loved her from the start."

As I did you, I thought, and looked away.

"All right. But you could be better employed. You could be living . . . What shall I tell Mother? She wants to see you, expects me to bring you back, if only for a visit."

"I want to see her, too," I said sincerely. "Tell her to come to Yonder."

I rose, for Zoé herself had risen and was leaving her palm tree earlier than usual, not going toward the tide line, but half running, half flying farther along the curve of beach.

"I must stop her," I said, and ran, too.

She had done this once before and I had had trouble in bringing her back. Was it her idea to gain the bay side by skirting the island? A long trip. More likely she had become conscious of my watching her—a thing she always forgot on leaving me—and planned to enter the water out of my sight. Soon the big sapodilla trees would hide her. Beyond them were coral reefs and rocks. I knew how quickly she could dive and disappear.

Dane was running with me, so I was less afraid.

Almost at the trees she lost a slipper. We gained on her while she retrieved it.

"Zoé!" I screamed, but she flew on.

"She mustn't get out of sight," I panted, and Dane ran on ahead of me.

"Zoé!" we called together, then Dane alone, almost at her side.

"Zoé!"

She stopped at that as if she had heard us for the first time. She turned, then came slowly back to meet us. I went toward her, but she was looking at Dane. I had never seen that look on her face. It was less a look than a light. She held out her hands.

"Skee!" she said.

She went up to him, put her arms about his neck. Automatically he embraced her, and she clung to him.

"We'll go right away," she was saying. "Where's the boat? Oh, Skee, we'll go right away."

We walked back along the beach, her hands clasped about his arm, her face lifted to his, rapturous in the belief that he was Skee. I was glad that he did nothing, said nothing, to disillusion her.

"You're late," she said, disturbed by his silence. "I was afraid something had happened to you. Oh, Skee, if anything happens to divide us . . . Talk to me. Aren't we going now?"

"Yes," he answered. "Yes, of course."

I was walking behind them, carrying the coat he had flung off as he started running. I remember that it was a white coat, and that he wore a blue shirt and tie. I remember that the sun lit up his hair, and that Zoé's hair shone with the same brightness, falling around her shoulders as it had done the night I saw her first. A thought came to me. Those two, so alike. Could it be . . . ? Impossible, I thought. But I felt faint.

Suddenly Zoé stopped and said, "I'm not going into the house, Skee. You shan't talk to Johanna. You shan't."

He was silent, putting on his coat, leaving me to manage her.

"We must go in, Zoé," I said. "You must change your dress. Something suitable," playing the game with her, as I had always played it.

She looked at Dane.

"Yes," said Dane. "If you're going with me, you must wear something suitable."

"We won't see Miss Johanna," I assured her as she still held back. "We'll go straight upstairs."

She came then. We went into the porte-cochère, into the house. She looked up and down the hall.

"It's all right," she said to Dane. "I'll run up and change my dress."

Dane said as she went toward the stair, "What a life for you, Olive."

He spoke as if Zoé were not there, or as if she were deaf, a trick Nannine had, and even Judge Croome at times. It always worried me, for Zoé missed nothing.

"What a life, Olive," said Dane. "Yet you'd rather live it than marry me."

Zoé's hand was on the balustrade. She stopped, looking from Dane to me. She half whispered,

"What did you say, Skee?"

I went to her side.

"Nothing, Zoé," I said. "Go on upstairs. I'm coming."

She pushed past me, went up to Dane, grasped his sleeve.

"Skee!" she whispered. "What did you say?"

I knew he had not understood, had not realized what the moment meant to her. I learned afterward that he had supposed she called any stranger Skee, expecting to go away with him. I motioned him to silence, wondering all the while if Zoé would remember the outcome of this day's vigil, if dealing with her would be more complicated now.

Dane ignored my signals, looked down into her eyes. He smiled, seeming to speak for my benefit, yet with some notion, too, of appealing to my patient, winning her sympathy and help.

"I love your Olive," he said. "I want to marry her and take her away. Tell her you don't need her, not the way I need her. Somebody else will do for you, but not for me. Tell her that."

Her hand fell from his sleeve. Staring at him, she screamed, her hands knotted over her heart, her eyes wide and startled, staring into his.

I put my arms around her, astonished that she did not drive

me off. A convulsion passed through her. She covered her face.

"He didn't mean it, Zoé," I said. "Tell her you didn't mean it," I implored Dane.

And Dane, contritely, "Don't worry, Zoé. I won't take her away. She won't come."

Ezra appeared out of the shadows. His low voice addressed us all.

"Miss Johanna wishes to see you." The old refrain.

"I'll be going," Dane remarked. "I'll write you, Olive."

"Pardon me, sir." Ezra stood between him and the outer door. "It was especially you Miss Johanna wished to see. Miss Zoé and Miss York, too, but especially you. She's in Judge Croome's room."

I disliked taking Zoé to Miss Johanna in such a state, though I believed Judge Croome's presence would insure harmony. I wanted to get her upstairs, back among familiar things, set her to playing with her phonograph, her shells, set her to forgetting. I had never seen her like this, wrung by an emotion so deep, yet, after that one scream, so quiet. I felt her shaking inside my arm as we went toward Miss Johanna. Dane came, too, prepared no doubt to offer his apologies for the night before. Would she forgive him? I doubted it.

Judge Croome sat propped up in bed, a broken, wasted figure, trying to smile a welcome, his eyes moving to Dane who stepped at once to his side, greeting him, taking the unsteady hand, while Ezra, hovering near, looked on.

Dane had bowed to Miss Johanna, and she had given him a clipped, unsmiling nod. She sat in her wheel chair, dressed in an outmoded gray gown that I had never seen, her hair drawn up into a knot that added to her height. She wore, too, the sapphire brooch and earrings of the day before.

Nannine stood behind her as if ready for some emergency.

"Sit down," Miss Johanna said to us all, and indicated the chair beside her, and the small carved love seat that had been brought from the judge's office adjoining.

Zoé and I took the love seat, Zoé silent, the tears running from her closed eyelids. I held to her hand, feeling it grow cold and rigid, feeling all her body grow rigid, as if she had died. Only her tears seemed alive. Miss Johanna appeared to notice nothing wrong.

Dane did not sit down, said that he hadn't time, must get on to Miami. I think he would have stayed and talked to Judge Croome, but found Miss Johanna too formidable for comfort. Certainly he didn't mention having ignored her dinner.

Miss Johanna pointed to the vacant chair.

"Sit down," she commanded him.

Zoé opened her eyes.

"No, Skee, no!" she cried. "Go while you can. Go, Skee! Go!"

"Skee?" said Miss Johanna, and poor Judge Croome looked from one to the other of them, not speaking, not able to speak.

Zoé's tearful eyes moved to her sister for the first time since she had been in the room. "It's Johanna's voice," she said, "but it's not Johanna. That old woman is not Johanna . . . And who is that?" staring at Judge Croome.

I whispered to her that it was indeed Miss Johanna, and that the sick man was her father, while Miss Johanna who had not heard her, repeated like a broken record, "Skee—

Skee—" till Zoé, who sat close to Dane, whispered to him, "Go away, Skee! She'll kill you."

"Skee," said Miss Johanna, not hearing her, looking only at Dane who had stayed, as I knew he would. "You are very like him," she said. "Very like the man she stole. And why not, since he sired you?"

That was how she said it. Not, "He was your father." Nothing so kind. It would not have been in keeping with the hatred, the utter loathing, in her face.

So it was true, the suspicion, the almost revelation, that had come to me on the beach. It was true, and Dane stood looking at her, while Zoé mumbled to herself, understanding nothing, and Judge Croome, lying against his pillows, tried to speak, his face contorted, his hand shaking on the spread, while Ezra, beside him, like a shadow against the wall, bent over him.

Miss Johanna looked only at Dane.

"You knew you were adopted, didn't you?" she asked.

"Yes," his eyes said, and challenged her. "I knew. What then?" his eyes said.

He knew. But no one else. Not even Pony. Not even Fritz. Secret. His secret, blared out like that.

How she was enjoying it.

"They thought they fooled me," she said. "My father, Dr. Lowrie, Roger and Helen Carrington. I knew when they slipped you out three days old, and went with you a thousand miles away.

"That imbecile is your mother," she said, pointing at Zoé. "I'll wager they didn't tell you that. Nor that your father did right to kill himself, however accidentally, and that she deserved to watch him die. Ezra came on them. He had come on them before. You have nothing to be proud of in your parents. Tell him, Ezra, what you found that night."

And Ezra, standing beside Judge Croome, replied,

"I found him in the grove with Miss Zoé, his rifle still in his hand."

"It's a lie," said Zoé quietly. "Johanna killed him."

Miss Johanna twisted in her chair to stare at Zoé.

"You did it last night," said Zoé, still quietly, meeting those blazing eyes. "It was Father who shot him, but it was you who nagged him into doing it, torturing him with tales Ezra had brought you, talking about my honor—I heard you. Last night, after I left Skee, I heard voices, I saw the lantern . . . I ran back . . . And Father—Father—"

She put her hands over her ears, closed her eyes.

"The sound— The sound— It split the earth . . . And Skee fell, and lay on the ground, and I ran to him. I held him in my arms. He spoke to me. He said, 'I love you.' He made me promise— He made me promise— I can't remember. Oh God! . . . Skee . . . Skee . . ."

Her voice sank, died. Her lips moved on.

"She's crazy," whispered Miss Johanna, while Judge Croome sat with his head fallen forward, not trying now to speak, and Dane stood like a man under a spell.

"I'm not crazy," Zoé flared up. "It's you who are crazy, saying this man is my child. Only an idiot would say such a thing. And what has happened to you—to both of you—that you look so terrible? Is it because you murdered Skee? Is it because you know what will happen to you now?"

What none of us realized was that Zoé had come back. The

213

shattering blow of Dane's words to me had opened a crevice in her mind, and light was streaming in. She still did not remember the year of violence, the birth of her child, nor any of the after years. Perhaps these, too, would move into the light as that last moment in the grove had done.

She stood up slowly, looking at Miss Johanna.

"Give me my brooch," she said in a low voice. "Give me my earrings."

She crossed the room while Miss Johanna drew back in her chair. Zoé wrenched the brooch from her throat. Miss Johanna covered her ears, and Nannine and I met in an effort to draw Zoé away, but Zoé was determined, and twisted like a cat.

Miss Johanna removed the earrings and gave them to her. She motioned in the direction of her father, silently indicating the state he was in, ordering us to go. Judge Croome lay with closed eyes, the breath fluttering in his throat. Ezra still hovered near him.

The play had not gone precisely as Miss Johanna had intended.

Dane opened the door for us, and we went out into the hall. I had meant to ask him not to leave at once, but as Zoé and I went toward the stair he came with us, and I realized that in the difficult time ahead we would have his help.

On the second floor Zoé said, "I'm going to my room," and, leaving us, went down the hall and opened the door of the room I had slept in that first night. I did not stop her. Perhaps it would be easier there.

She looked from Dane to me as we went in with her. Dane opened a window, letting in the fresh air. I closed the door.

"Who are you?" she asked me coldly.

I told her that I was Olive, and that I had been there for more than a year.

"I have not seen you before," she said.

She glanced again at Dane.

"You look like Skee," she said in a low voice. "Except— his hair was darker. His eyes were darker, too. It was the lashes made them dark. Dark lashes."

She looked down at her hands, at her skirt, almost as if she feared what she might see. Was this the dress that she had worn that night? Pale and quiet, she turned to the window Dane had opened, stood looking at the beach she had left an hour before.

"I thought I would die if Skee died," she said, half to herself. "I swore I would drown myself if I couldn't have Skee. We both swore to die if anything— But last night before he went he made me promise not to keep that vow . . . What have they done with him?" she asked, looking from one to the other of us. "Did they take him away?"

Dane answered yes, they had taken him away.

You were strangely gentle, Dane, strangely kind. Had they evaded your questions all your life? Were you glad the questions were over, you who had once said, thinking of your own clouded birth, that natural children were the better children? Did the tale Johanna Croome had told you answer those questions so completely that you accepted it without a doubt?

He stood beside the big stone fireplace, an elbow on the mantel, smoking, nervous, abstracted, yet gentle, too.

"Who took him?" Zoé asked softly, looking at me.

"His family," I hazarded.

215

She repeated the words, looking at Dane, believing him, no doubt, some cousin or brother of Skee's.

She was composed and still, yet for her Skee had died only the night before. Long after, speaking of Zoé's case, a psychiatrist of note said to me, "Remember that the knowledge of Skee's death had lain in her subconscious a long time. It was not actually new to her, and yet a violent reaction would not have been surprising."

I looked for violence at any moment.

She sank beside me on the sofa, sat there spent, such sadness as I had never imagined on her face. It was plain that though she felt we were there to comfort her, she would have preferred to be alone.

And yet I dared not leave her alone.

XXII

We sat at coffee in Richard's house, Dane and Zoé and I.

Luncheon we had eaten in Zoé's old room. I had served it there myself by the simple procedure of going up to the tower and waiting for it to arrive on the dumb-waiter. I knew that the machinery of the house would be going on as usual, though I wondered about the judge and Miss Johanna. How disturbed they must be, knowing that Zoé had come back, that the truth about Skee's death had at last been told. Miss Johanna had not denied that truth except to mumble for the thousandth time perhaps, "She's crazy."

How malignant her eyes had been when they rested now and then on me. No doubt she was blaming me now for Zoé's return. Ezra would have been in earshot when the three of us came from the beach into the hall, would have heard what Dane said to me, and later, or even then, would have discovered her hallucination regarding him. But Miss Johanna would say that I had been hammering on that rock for many months, and that Dane's words were merely the final blow.

Perhaps, however, they were so distracted by Zoé's revelations that they could think little about Zoé herself.

I brought the luncheon downstairs, spread it on the small table from which I had eaten my first repast in Croome Castle. There was abundance, as always, though none of us was hungry. Afterward I persuaded Zoé to get into a kimono and lie down on the bed.

Dane had gone out. From the window I could see him walking along the beach, stopping now and then to look out across the water, as I had seen him do as a child. He walked slowly, on and on, past the jetty and beyond the big sapodilla trees . . .

Zoé was weeping. Now that Dane was gone she wept almost as if she were alone. She spoke Skee's name, sobbing to think that her father could have done this thing, only it was Johanna who had really done it. "And I will tell the world when the time comes. I will lay my hand on the Bible and tell the world."

"But it was long ago," I said. "Don't grieve now, or tell anybody. It was years ago."

"No, no!" she cried. "It would drive me crazy if I believed that. And Johanna—did you hear her say that man is my son? What's the matter with her? Everybody's crazy. I'll go crazy, too."

I was silent, realizing how perilous was the height she had climbed. A touch might send her back into the abyss. She was asleep when Dane returned, and I asked him to sit with her. I wanted to see Richard, talk with him, tell him what had happened.

The downstairs was ominously still. Through a vista of rooms I saw Nannine dusting, moving about methodically. I went out of the house and along the beach road thinking that it was good for Dane and Zoé to be alone. Perhaps she would wake and they would talk together.

"Judge Croome," said Richard. "The judge . . . Who would have believed it? If you had said Johanna . . . And yet . . ."

He stood silent, dumfounded by the turn of events.

"Dane and Zoé," he said after a moment. "How alike they are, when you know. Zoé . . . It may take years for her to come back all the way. She will have to believe, she will have to accept until she remembers."

"She refuses to believe. Why should she? She doesn't know us, and she would never believe Johanna. She says it would drive her crazy."

"We'll have Belen come," he answered. "I was sending for her anyway. You and Zoé were coming here this afternoon, remember? . . . No wonder you loved Zoé, since you had always loved Dane. Now you'll be leaving Yonder. Now you'll be going away."

"I have no plans," I said, "but to stay on with Zoé."

"But the man's in love with you. He told me so. And he's asked you to marry him."

"I'm not going to do it," I said.

He smiled, standing there beside his typewriter, beside the work I had interrupted. I hardly know what was in the smile —incredulity, an amused patience with a woman's dallying and caprice.

I turned away from him, went out the door and back along the beach road.

Zoé was awake, was talking with Dane.

"They call you Dane," she was saying. "I have a cousin, Helen Dane. Helen Dane Carrington. Do you know her?"

He replied that he did, that they lived in the same town.

"But Helen lives here," she answered. "Helen lives in Muspa."

She noticed that I had come in, and I asked her if later she would go with me to Richard's house, realizing that she would not know who Richard was. "Belen will be there," I added.

She lay still for a while, then got out of bed and went into the bathroom. "My things are not in there," she came out to say. "My cream, my powder . . ." She went to the closet, opened it on empty rods and shelves.

"Your clothes are in the tower," I said.

"Who took them there?" she demanded.

"Perhaps you yourself," I answered. "Or Belen. It was before I came. I don't know who took them there."

"Belen might have done it," she agreed. "Belen was going to send them to me after I'd gone. I was taking only a few—in a satchel. It's under the bed there."

She began to sob again.

Dane said that he would meet us at Richard's house, and left. Zoé went with me up the stair. In the tower she looked about her, anger for a moment submerging her tears.

"Who moved my drawing table?" she asked. "And where are all my paints? Those books . . . Where are the books I used to study?"

She looked at the dressing table, at the combs and brushes and perfume bottles she had left in orderly arrangement on its glass surface.

"That mirror belongs in Mama's dressing room," she said, as if to herself. "Those shells—who did that? Miss Anderson's chair has new cushions. She used to teach us, sitting in that chair. Her desk was where that wardrobe is, and Johanna's desk and my desk were here . . . That bed. Why did they take it out of the north guest room?"

She went to the door that had been mine, went down the step, came back to say,

"Johanna's piano is gone." She was looking at me now. "I was up here only last week," she said, "while Johanna was in New York buying her trousseau. Everything was just as it was when these were our schoolrooms. Mama ordered them kept that way. She used to come up here and watch—out that window—the way I've watched for Skee . . . I know why. I've found her letters. No matter . . . Someone's been living in these rooms. Is it you?"

"You and I both, Zoé. And before that, you and Susan."

"Why do you lie to me?" she asked. "Why does everyone lie to me? Isn't it enough that Skee— Isn't it enough that I want to die? Why must you say these things to me?"

"Because you wouldn't want to die if you realized it was all over long ago. Belen will tell you the same."

She was silent, and I saw that she was gazing into the mirror above the dressing table, gazing at her own face, young and lovely under its cloud of shining hair. How could it have been long ago, the lucent blue-green eyes inquired, gazing back into hers.

"Belen does not lie to me," she said, turning away.

She went to the cedrella chest at the foot of the bed, raised its lid. On top of the napkins and doilies I had laid the dresses that she had discarded when the new ones came from Mrs. Frisbie. She saw these, and closed the chest, supposing no doubt that they belonged to whoever had occupied the rooms.

She opened the wardrobe and began to take out the newer dresses, to lay them on the bed. Now and then she paused to look at one more closely, as if it had in some way changed, but the mystery did not engage her long.

I persuaded her to dress there in the tower.

"But why am I going? I can't see anyone. Why should I go?"

"Belen will be there."

At last she bathed her face, brushed her hair, got into a white dimity dress she had seldom worn. We went downstairs through the still house and along the beach road. It was almost dusk. Rory came to greet us, to solicit Zoé's caress, but she drew away from him. "Whose house is that?" she demanded at sight of Richard's place. "There's no house there. There can't be."

She grew frantic, and would have turned back, would have wept, but that she saw Richard coming toward us. He was a stranger, and she composed herself.

I introduced them. It seemed the right thing to do.

Richard was a stranger. Dane and me she barely knew. Now in her sorrow she sat with us in this incredible house, waiting for Belen. Belen was the only friend she had.

"Here they are," Richard said, as Floyd and Belen came up

the walk. He went to meet them, and presently Belen stood in the door, leaning on her cane, blinking her aged eyes.

It was not until she spoke that Zoé knew her.

"I've told her to tell Zoé everything," Richard said, as we walked outside, leaving Belen and Dane and Zoé together.

We went down by the bay, quiet tonight under the early stars.

"She'll believe Belen," Richard added. "She's got to believe. Otherwise—"

"Otherwise what?" I said. "Can't she go on as she is?"

"She'd go insane," he answered. "Imagine the changes she'll find in the world."

"In the world. Not in Yonder."

"No, not in Yonder. But Dane will take her away."

I hadn't thought of that. "Are you sure?" I asked.

"No, but he implied as much when I delegated my guardianship of Zoé to him. Why should he leave her with Johanna?"

Why, indeed? Of course he would take her away.

"And you, Olive," stopping beside the pier. "You said your plans were to stay on with Zoé. You said you wouldn't go with Dane, wouldn't marry him. I couldn't believe you. I thought, I'll wait and see. I'd go on waiting, I thought, though I don't wait easily. Remember the first night we went to the Barnacle, and you told me about Dane?"

"Yes."

"Remember what I said? No, you've forgotten that. I said if a man came to your door the ghost would drive him away. Who wants a woman all full of ghost?"

"Did you come to my door?"

"I was at your door from the first."

"And turned away?"

"Yes, but I took you with me, you and your disturbing eyes. Whether I was asleep or awake, at home or on the mid-Atlantic, there you were. There you'll always be. I can't wait to see whether you'll go with Dane and Zoé, or start off on some tack of your own. I don't want you to go at all. I want to hold you, to take that rope there and tie you to the piling, wrap it round and round you, like Joan at the stake."

In the starlight I looked into his face. There was no smile in his eyes.

"I'm tied to Yonder already," I said.

"But to me, Olive," grasping my hands. "Tied to me. For always."

The earth stood still.

"For always," I said, and knew that nothing else would do.

I sometimes forget that this is Zoé's story. Zoé's and Dane's . . .

I don't know when Zoé first came to believe, to understand. During that long evening with Dane and Belen while Richard and I walked along the bay shore and talked about the future, I know that she came to accept, to consent to the tale that Skee had been dead for thirty years, that Dane was her son.

That night I saw the shadow cross her face. Even before she said to me, "I am old," I saw the shadow. She was standing before the glass in her room downstairs, and I saw. Nothing so definite as a line or a change of contour. It was merely as if a gray veil had dropped over her.

"I am old," she said.

And before the week was out I saw the fading of her hair.

XXIII

Late that night Dane left for Miami to be gone three days. The next day Nannine came to me while I was clearing things out of the tower. Zoé had refused to stay anywhere but in her old room, had slept there the night before. I had asked Nannine to have Stella prepare the room next to it for me—a room separated only by the bath—and she had complied with no suggestion that Miss Johanna might object.

Judge Croome was dying, she told me now. Dr. Gordon of Muspa was with him, but what could anyone do? "We might have expected it after yesterday," she said.

Dying. The miasma of the house seemed heavier.

I asked her how Miss Johanna was taking it.

"She hasn't left his side," Nannine answered. "Mr. Lowrie's there, too. The old man don't know a thing."

No one sent for Zoé to come down. She slept peacefully that night, waking to receive the news of her father's death. I remember her white and tearless face as I gave her that news, and how she turned from me, sealed and withdrawn, though she had once admitted me to her inmost thoughts.

White and tearless still, she walked beside Dane at the funeral. We went on foot along the hard coral path to the ancient Croome burying ground, almost at the center of the key. It was a desolate spot, shut off from the sun by interlocking trees, by walls of vine and shrubbery. Gray headstones stood around us, and high on a dead branch a lone bald eagle looked down, like the spirit of the judge at his own funeral.

I can still see Miss Johanna, her dark veil thrown back, leading the procession of family and servants; can still see the yellow pallor of her face in the sunlight, her black-clad figure erect in the wheel chair, carefully propelled by Ezra. At her request, Richard read the burial service. For some reason, she had not wanted a minister of the Gospel present, yet remembered perhaps the days when the judge had been a good churchman. I had taken to Richard a white prayerbook that Nannine brought from the attic. "She had others," Nannine said, "but I think she burned them."

Richard's voice sounded like Father's as he read the words of sorrow and relinquishment. Zoé, beside Dane, seemed not to listen, not to be there at all.

I glanced at Miss Johanna.

She had dropped her veil over her face.

Richard was present at the reading of Judge Croome's will, made three years before. Johanna, by a rule of primogeniture in the family, became heir to Yonder. There was a bequest to Roger and Helen Carrington, and a smaller one to Richard who was appointed Zoé's guardian. The rest of the old man's wealth was divided equally between Johanna and Zoé. Johanna was named executrix.

Zoé said to Dane when they came upstairs,

"Everything in this room is mine. It was not left to Johanna, and I'm taking it all with me."

At the funeral Zoé had worn for the last time one of the long dresses that Mrs. Frisbie had made for her—the light green muslin that I associated with the hurricane and our visit to the buried chapel. I would have advised her to wear white that day, but she had not asked my advice and I hesitated to offer it to the stranger she had become. The dress had not looked out-of-place, but had seemed to mingle with the leaves, to furnish almost a protective coloring. Her closed white face was all you seemed to see.

Dane had bought her a small overnight bag, a fitted suitcase and a wardrobe trunk. Now as they prepared to leave she packed at his insistence only the clothes she had worn before I "found" the others. Many of these were beautiful, and he promised to get her more. He chose from among them a gray and blue print for her to travel in, and I gave her a hat she had always admired. If I was going to stay on Yonder, I had no need of hats.

Dane had asked me nothing about my own plans, yet surely —now that Zoé no longer needed me—he must have wondered what they were. I knew that I must tell him about Richard and me. Perhaps he wouldn't care. He seemed different now.

He followed me up to the tower while Zoé with Stella's help was packing. I had gone to recover some odds and ends, and take them down to Richard's house. Dane took the light basket I was carrying, and went with me up the stair.

In the tower he stood looking out the barred window, thinking, I imagined, of Zoé and her long years in this room, or of the times when he had visited her here as a child.

Presently he said,

"The wild Croome blood. You're wise not to tie up with it."

"It's not all wild," I answered.

"Yes, it is. Wild and mad. And the Croomes always miss love. It's a tradition. They miss love by a hair's breadth or a mile, by fate or their own clumsiness." He turned and looked at me where I stood with my basket of trinkets and books and bottles of perfume.

"Lowrie's so right for you," he said. "You're a wise girl."

"It wasn't wisdom," I answered, taken aback.

"I can believe that," he said. "I saw your face when you came up from the pier the night we talked with Belen. That's how I knew. But sometimes love makes an intuitive selection, that's wisdom, isn't it? And that was how I lost you. The real thing came along. You might have told me."

"I didn't know," I said.

He smiled. "You told me once that was impossible—to love and not know it."

"I mean I didn't know about *him*. Oh, Dane, let's not analyze."

"You used to be a bear for analysis."

"What I mean is, he never gave me any sign—any that meant—any that couldn't be just friendship. Not till he knew I wasn't going to marry you. He said I was full of a ghost."

"Meaning me, I suppose. So I'm a ghost."

"He said that because I told him I'd buried you."

"Thanks. It's a gruesome feeling."

"I hadn't, of course. You're vital and alive—in my memory and everywhere else."

"I'm comforted. But I wouldn't have asked you again to marry me. Not now, knowing what I know."

I thought he referred to the circumstances of his birth. Surely he had suspected that he might have been what he had once called a natural child. Yes, undoubtedly he had suspected, and had built his own defense against it. Was the defense failing him now?

"The Croome blood," he added. "There's a taint in it. I never knew what blood I had, but I felt sorry for Fritz and Pony, even for Mother—their mother. It was your father steadied *her*, his influence somehow—she said it was his sermons. I always suspected she loved him—a little more than you're exhorted to love your neighbor, or your parson. No matter."

He turned to the window again. "You're going to be happy with Lowrie," he added. "You may be lonesome years on end, or you may take to the seas with him and drown. But you'll be happy. I wouldn't want your children to be Croomes. It's bad enough for Dorilys and the rest of us. Where we'll end I can't imagine. I told you, didn't I, that Fritz had joined the Marines?"

"Is that bad?"

"At his age, yes."

He came over to me, leaned down, and as if in fun, lightly kissed my eyebrow.

"Lucky Lowrie," he said, and took my basket, and opened the door.

Dane and Zoé left next morning, Zoé less pale than she had been of late, her hair knotted smoothly below the small hat with its wreath of rose-apples. There was quite a scene before they left.

I had been in earlier to see Miss Johanna and give an entirely superfluous notice, as well as thank her for my salary check which she had sent me in full by Nannine, though the month was only half gone.

She appeared to be dressed for visitors—formally, in one of her many black dresses, her gray hair arranged neatly, her face seeming more gaunt, more grim than usual.

No thanks were called for, she informed me. In paying my salary she was doing no more than she had contracted to do. And she had known, of course, that I would not remain since her sister was leaving.

I had turned away when she added in the same voice,

"I should like to thank you for your kindness to my father."

This surprised me, since she had once appeared to misinterpret what she called my kindness. I murmured something about having liked him, and added a blundering word of sympathy.

She was silent, then she said,

"Richard Lowrie tells me he's marrying you."

"Yes," I answered.

"This afternoon," she said.

"Yes."

She was to surprise me still more.

"Would you like," she asked, "to be married here? You may have the parlors, the music room—any you like."

I explained that Richard had made the arrangements—at some church. "He knows the parson," I added lamely.

She seemed disappointed, but I could not have my wedding in the fogs of that house. Perhaps in the tower. But Miss Johanna could not come to the tower, if she had intended coming.

"Good-by," I said, and she gave me her clipped nod.

Her parting with Dane and Zoé was even less genial—a scene, in fact.

Zoé had been determined to take with her the furnishings of her room. She and Dane did not consult Richard about this, and whether or not any intercession on his part would have helped, I don't know. The moving men simply came from Muspa—belatedly, the morning Zoé was to leave—and Miss Johanna, propelled by Ezra, met them in the hall, forbidding them to proceed. Dane stated that they were there by his orders, that the objects in question were not a part of Yonder but belonged to Zoé personally.

Miss Johanna sat at the stairfoot as silent and erect as when Ezra had steered her under the trees behind her father's coffin. When Dane ordered the men to go ahead, they looked at Miss Johanna and left, even though Zoé appeared and begged them to take at least the breakfront. I learned afterward that later attempts were made through a lawyer, but with no more success.

That encounter in the hall was the last time Miss Johanna was to see her sister. Zoé went back to her room, and together we stowed in her luggage the silver clock and crystal vases, all other ornaments, what paintings we could, and the fittings of the desk. Richard helped Dane get the trunk downstairs and strap it to the car. They carried out the bags.

The house was deserted as we went down, but Nannine waited in the porte-cochère to kiss Zoé good-by, and Stella waved from the shrubbery of the drive.

We drove Dane and Zoé to the ferry, watched them go.

They stood at the rail, waving back, looking like sister and brother, like bride and groom.

Zoé—going out into the world.

"She'll find changes," I said. "And she'll change, too."

"She would change on Yonder," Richard answered.

"If only she could hold her youth," I said. "She's held it so long. If only she knew how."

"Will you hold yours?" asked Richard. "Will I? Would we bother? . . . Right now I'm thinking about this afternoon."

They call it the Sailors' Chapel. A light burns in its steeple all night. When there is fog, its heavy bronze and gold bell rings continually, an ancient bell that came from Spain by way of Cuba and was found in an old sugar mill where it used to call the slaves to work. More than once when the wind was right I had heard that bell sounding from the mainland coast, and little knew it would ring for my own wedding.

It was ringing when we came from the launch. Nannine

233

and Floyd were with us, and a few strangers who had strayed into the pews. Nannine had taken an interest, was delighted that I had among my possessions a white crepe dress, scarcely worn; had herself gone into Muspa to bring back a wedding veil and a wreath of fresh orange blossoms. I remember Richard dark and handsome in his white suit, a rose from my bouquet in his buttonhole. I remember the parson's voice and the organ's solemn peal, and Nannine crying in the front pew because she always did at weddings.

Gulls circled about us as we went down to the pier. They circled because they hoped for food, but to me with my bridal thoughts their wings seemed beautiful, like happy omens.

XXIV

I was to see Zoé and Dane again in five years from the day we parted, to see Pony, too—all of them except Fritz. Richard and I were about to sail for Guam which would be my third voyage in the *Chantey*. There had been a belated wedding trip to Eleuthera, and a book about it, followed by a delicious summer, a pleasant fall and a grisly winter on Attu, at the end of the Aleutian chain. *World's End* came of that. And now we were setting out for Guam which at that time still kept traces of Agaua, its ancient city, and the lost race of the Chamorros. However, a telegram came from Pony saying that she was visiting her parents and wanted to see us. Guam could do nothing but wait.

Pony had changed little. She had more poise, and her clothes, to which she had always been indifferent, were the final word; but she was still Pony, lively and unpredictable. The baron had died, and she was married now to a bullfighter from Seville, a young man with somber eyes and black silk hair and the grace of a cat. Her father hated him, but the rest of us found him magnetic.

Zoé lived with Dane and Dorilys in the house Leonie had built. For some time she had been remembering early events of the dark years. They returned to her, she told me, in what seemed to be a chronological sequence, sparsely at times, then crowding fast. "It's like remembering dreams," she said. "Sometimes they're cloudy, sometimes clear."

She had not progressed to a memory of Richard or Susan, though Nannine had come dimly into focus, only to fade away. She recalled no moments of frenzy or violence.

"Most often," she said, "I remember giving my music box and my ping-pong set to a little boy, and his mother making him give them back. The woman was Helen, and the child, she says, was Dane . . . Then again I am standing at a window, and Johanna is daring me to jump. And I *want* to jump . . . But that must have been a dream. They said then it was a dream."

Her hair was quite gray and faded. There were lines in her face, and the firm contour of her throat was gone. She looked old, "But not so old as the rest of us," Helen Carrington said. She still wore the little bull's-eye watch, and I thought how she had said she was going to will it to me, and how it had once symbolized for me Zoé herself. She had forgotten that promise now, and all our days together, would perhaps never arrive at them.

Dorilys was dark like Leonie, but she had a spirituelle quality that had belonged to Zoé, and her features were Dane's. "I hope not," Dane said. "The Roys aren't saints and geniuses, but I hope she stays on that side."

It was sixteen years before I saw Dane again.

We were still living on Yonder when we visited the Carringtons. During those five years I had come into little contact with Miss Johanna, perhaps twice a year when she had Richard and me to dinner. Richard called on her now and then, for she liked to discuss the farm with him. Nannine left while we were on Guam, and after that, for some reason, Miss Johanna never asked us to dinner.

After Guam we bought a place in Muspa, one with a widow's walk on top so that I might watch for my seafaring man. There was plenty of watching in the years that followed. Our three children began to arrive, and while they were small I stayed ashore. When I sailed again it was in our new ketch, the *Inca*, a larger boat than the *Chantey*, and we took our older boy. That was *Tahiti*, the most adventurous of our trips.

We often went with the children to spend week ends on Yonder, and Richard, still paying his respects to Miss Johanna, found her growing more grim and taciturn with the years. Always beside her was Ezra, and, hovering not far away, the girl, Stella. Zoé was living in Paris where Dane had full charge of the Roy interests, and Dorilys had gone on the stage. Pony, oddly enough, was still married to her bullfighter (retired now) and living in Seville.

This was the *status quo* when we sailed for Tahiti. When we came back it was to learn that Miss Johanna had died a month before. The event caused some commotion because she had left everything she had to Ezra. This included, of course, Yonder Key.

Friends informed us of these things at once, and that afternoon we were visited by Ezra's attorney. Ezra wished to buy

Richard's house on Yonder and the plot of ground on which it stood. It seemed that in his youth Ezra had married a Seminole woman and was now father, grandfather, and great grandfather of a family or tribe that desired the key to themselves.

Reserving action, we telephoned Helen Carrington and learned that Zoé planned to contest Miss Johanna's will. She had supposed that as next in line her inheritance of Yonder would be automatic, and she had written in her own will that she left her rights in Yonder to Dane. Zoé had been ill—some coronary trouble—but as soon as she was able she would return.

However, Zoé died the night before she was to sail. Dying, she exacted of Dane a promise to come in her stead, to identify himself in the Florida courts and break Johanna's will.

Dane knew, of course, that born outside the law of parents who had not afterward married, he had no rights of his own, but he had promised, and he came. Roger and Helen Carrington came, too—Belen had died years before. Ezra also took the stand, and under the questioning of his lawyer, his version of the old scandal was laid bare, a sordid tale of loose love, of faithless bridegroom and treacherous younger sister, of a father's vengeance on the seducer, a bride's broken heart, her ruined life and lonely death—no one at her side, indeed, except the old servant who had been with her through it all. We wondered at this probing of the past, this exhuming of a tragedy half a century old. Dane had made no claims except through his mother who had willed her "rights" to him, and who might have recovered Yonder had she lived.

I can see Dane now, sitting in the judge's chambers, distinguished looking in his middle age, his hair seeming to have darkened as it turned gray, his mouth to have firmed. There was not then, nor before, nor after, any sign that he felt his birth a stigma. Somehow, long ago, he had worked the problem out, and abode with the conclusions he had reached.

The village of Muspa felt otherwise, and stared curiously. At any rate, there he was, the older ones remarked; Zoé had not murdered her child. And they had suspected that the young violin teacher had not died by accident—they knew Judge Croome. Under the circumstances, his act was a natural one.

Dane did not feel the loss of Yonder as Zoé had felt it. To him, the key and its farm would have been more care than comfort. Before they left we took the three of them—Roger and Helen Carrington and Dane—for a cruise in the Bahamas. Dane and I were thrown often together in a solitude of sea and sky, a solitude in which he talked to me freely. It was only for Zoé's sake that he regretted Yonder.

"Did she look old at the last?" I asked him.

"Yes," he said. "Like anybody else at seventy-five. And frail. Hers was a strange case. I wonder how your father would have explained it."

"I think he would have said what Richard says, that Zoé was locked in one moment of time for thirty years, proving that time is mental, which we know—it's just so strange to see it proved."

Darkness was spreading over the water. There were clouds and a few stars. I could hardly see Dane's face.

"Queer," he said, "the things that stick in your mind. I once heard your father preach a sermon on the text, 'There *shall be time no longer.'* He classed time with disease and death and crime—yes, and grief. All tears would be wiped away. It would be here on earth, not in some faraway heaven, and it would be sooner than we think. But first the great dragon would swell itself to undreamed-of size, the great dragon of all evil that started out as a little serpent in Eden, a little coaxing snake that might have been stepped on and killed . . . Are you listening, Olive?"

"Of course I'm listening. I don't remember that sermon."

"You were very small, and probably dreaming in your pew the way you did sometimes. I listened. I remember it."

He had listened, a young boy, his attention fixed by that picture of the dragon swelling itself in vain. And now he remembered.

"Have you forgotten," he said, "what an irresponsible generation we were in the twenties, bitter little iconoclasts, blaming our parents for the rotten world we lived in. Now we ourselves have given our children an even worse world. Men's hearts failing them for fear. You as a mother of sons fearing most of all. Youth can be anything but irresponsible now. Wars and rumors of wars. The dragon swelling still, knowing that his time is short, and the bottomless pit just ahead. I had always thought it was us sinners that were headed for the bottomless pit, but it was the dragon . . . Fragments of what he said come back to me. *'For we wrestle not against flesh and blood, but . . . against powers, against the rulers of the darkness of this world. . . .' 'these things must come to pass . . . see that ye be not troubled . . .' 'Underneath are the everlasting arms.'* . . . Strange how things fasten themselves in your mind, things that seemed hardly to impress you at the time."

Strange, yes, a message from Father across the dark water. I asked Dane once if Zoé had ever remembered me, if in her journey back through the fog she had ever arrived at our year together. I hoped somehow she had, for I had loved her. He answered, "I told her about you long ago, what you meant to me. So she knew about you. As for her memories of that time, she seldom spoke of those."

So Yonder was given back to the Indians. I understand that among themselves they call it by an Indian name, perhaps the old one of Chassahowitska. Sailing past the key you catch glimpses of their brightly clad figures moving among the trees, poling their cypress dugouts in the waterways, or darting about the bay in speed boats. Their small wall-less homes are scattered the length of Yonder, bundles tied under the rafters, shell heaps and kitchen middens in front.

What have they done with Croome Castle, I often wonder —with the ancient loot, the portraits, the rugs and tapestries; with the massive furniture, some of it very fine? Do the ghosts of old Jared Croome and his cronies still hold their wassail in the great banquet hall and the idols from the globe's four corners leer and wink in the buried chapel? Does anyone at all look through the barred windows of the tower? Ezra was used to the white man's houses, Ezra himself part white. Perhaps he reigns there alone. Not much farming is done on the key, we know that, with Hiram and his family gone.

But Richard's house. I wonder what use they make of that. And the grove. Do the bats haunt it still, and the swamp smell wrap you like a cloak, and the blood-red blossoms drip from their writhing, twisting vines? Does every planted thing die in it, and the unseen presence creep after you when you pass through its darkness, day or night?

One question, at least, was answered.

A month after Dane left, a small package came to me from Paris. Dane, executor of Zoé's will, had written across the card inside:

"She left you this."

It was the little bull's-eye watch.